Bolan chased the Mob chief into the carnival fun house

The Executioner found himself in a maze lined with mirrors. He charged forward, then noticed the passages were leading back toward the beginning.

Suddenly he looked up and saw Nazarione firing a .38. Bolan expected to feel the bite of hot lead. Instead he heard glass shattering to his right.

Pieces of mirror lay on both sides of the thin wall, and Bolan could see into the next aisle. He extended his hand and saw its reflection at the end of the passageway.

The warrior crept forward stealthily and waited. A moment later Nazarione appeared and raised his weapon, but did not fire. He watched as Bolan's distorted image lifted its gun, then stepped away from the mirror.

The capo gasped and fired the automatic. Too late. Three rounds from the 93-R ripped into his chest.

Bolan left the corpse and made his way to the exit. He nodded to the ticket taker.

'Too scary for me," Bolan said.

MACK BOLAN

The Executioner

DON PENDLETON's EXECUTIONER
MACK BOLAN

Baltimore Trackdown

A GOLD EAGLE BOOK FROM
W⊕RLDWIDE

TORONTO · NEW YORK · LONDON · PARIS
AMSTERDAM · STOCKHOLM · HAMBURG
ATHENS · MILAN · TOKYO · SYDNEY

First edition April 1986

ISBN 0-373-61088-2

Special thanks and acknowledgment to
Chet Cunningham for his contributions to this work.

Printed in Canada

Then one of the judges of the city stood forth and said, Speak to us of Crime and Punishment.
And he answered, saying:
It is when your spirit goes wandering upon the wind,
That you, alone and unguarded, commit a wrong unto others and therefore unto yourself.
And for that wrong committed must you knock and wait a while unheeded at the gate of the blessed.
— Kahlil Gibran, *The Prophet*

I believe that for my enemies the wait may be forever. Perhaps in the end even I will have to defend my actions. And yet, with that knowledge, I cannot turn my back on the innocent victims of evil.
— Mack Bolan

THE
MACK BOLAN
LEGEND

Nothing less than a war could have fashioned the destiny of the man called Mack Bolan. Bolan earned the Executioner title in the jungle hellgrounds of Vietnam, for his skills as a crack sniper in pursuit of the enemy.

But this supreme soldier also wore another name—Sergeant Mercy. He was so tagged because of the compassion he showed to wounded comrades-in-arms and Vietnamese civilians.

Mack Bolan's second tour of duty ended prematurely when he was given emergency leave to return home and bury his family. Bolan made his peace at his parents' and sister's gravesite. Then he declared war on the evil force that had snatched his loved ones. The Mafia.

In a fiery one-man assault, he confronted the Mob head-on, carrying a cleansing flame to the urban menace. And when the battle smoke cleared, a solitary figure walked away alive.

He continued his lone-wolf struggle, and soon a hope of victory began to appear. But Mack Bolan had broken society's every rule. That same society started gunning for this elusive warrior—to no avail.

So Bolan was offered amnesty to work within the system against international terrorism. This time, as an official employee of Uncle Sam, Bolan wore yet another handle: Colonel John Phoenix. With government sanction now, and a command center at Stony Man Farm in Virginia's Blue Ridge Mountains, he and his new allies—Able Team and Phoenix Force—waged relentless war on a new adversary: the KGB and all it stood for.

Until the inevitable occurred. Bolan's one true love, the brilliant and beautiful April Rose, died at the hands of the Soviet terror machine.

Embittered and utterly saddened by this feral deed, Bolan broke the shackles of Establishment authority.

Now the big justice fighter is once more free to haunt the treacherous alleys of the shadow world.

1

The tension was felt by every person around the poker table. Mack Bolan, wearing a dark-blue suit, contrasting silk tie and shiny black shoes, stood out of the circle of light where he could see everyone and not be too conspicuous. His right hand hovered near the Beretta in his waistband. There had been no way he could attach the silencer and still dress well enough to be admitted into this fancy casino.

The Executioner casually watched the three Mafia hardmen in the room, who were concentrating on the spectators rather than the game. Security was their job and Bolan had pegged them as Mafia enforcers the moment he had entered. About twenty people watched the game.

This was the "big money" back room of the Flamingo nightclub in downtown Baltimore, the newest, classiest club in town, where the moneyed set could dance and booze, and their elite gamble with the sky as limit. This was the Highball Room where only five-hundred-dollar chips were used. With a pair of hundred-dollar bills Bolan had persuaded two doormen to let him inside.

The stakes in the game of seven-card stud were climbing. The last bet, ten thousand dollars, had been matched and raised by an equal amount. Only two men were left in the game—a sunburned Texan with oil gushing out of his pockets and with a temper as hot as an oil-well fire, and the house man, Spur, small and dark with black inscrutable eyes, who could make the cards do magical things. But apparently not now.

The Texan leaned back in the padded swivel chair and yawned.

"God a'mighty, suh! You gonna make up your mind and call me or fold?"

Both hands lay face up on the table. The Texan, with a pair of aces and a pair of queens showing, could go full house easily. The house man had three sixes and a seven showing; it wasn't much of a start on a straight, but there was a chance one of his three hole cards might be the fourth six.

The woman behind the oil man, pretty but not beautiful, patted her face with a lace handkerchief. She watched impassively as the oil man consulted his three hole cards.

She touched the handkerchief to her upper lip.

The timing was too perfect for Bolan's suspicious mind. She could be totally innocent. Or she could be with the house, and the handkerchief could be concealing a small radio transmitter. She had seen the Texan's hidden cards. Did she somehow reveal them?

The house player wore a hearing aid. He shook his head, reached to his stack of chips, called and raised another twenty thousand.

"Bluffing me, you cotton-pickin' roadrunner!" the Texan growled. He shoveled the blue chips out. "Call you—let's see them."

The house man tapped his three sixes. "I've got you beaten on the board unless you can top three of a kind."

The Texan shrugged. "So what the hell—it was a good try. I didn't have my goddamned full house, not even three queens or aces. But how did you know that?"

Spur felt the tension rise. The Texan could afford to lose the seventy-five thousand he had dropped in that hand. But with more than a hundred fifty thousand on the table, the hardmen were going to be doubly watchful.

The Texan turned, grabbed the linen hankie from the girl behind him and opened it to find a transmitter smaller than a matchbook.

"Now how you-all gonna explain this?" the Texan shouted, his face red.

The house man froze. Two bouncer gorillas moved in beside the Texan. They were armed, Bolan was sure.

He saw the floor boss reaching down, and the Executioner knew the man was dipping toward a leg holster. Bolan drew the Beretta, tracking the two Mafia goons who had reached for hardware.

"Don't try it!" Bolan snarled. The floor boss straightened up, and the hardmen stopped, hands motionless inside jackets. "Freeze," Bolan shouted, "and no one will get hurt!" He pointed with the Beretta at the two hardmen and the house man at the table. "Three of you, hands in the air. The rest of you go out the back door. This place is closed. Now, move—no panic, just file out. My Texan friend can take the chips he was cheated of, if he wants to."

The Texan divided the pot, pocketed one half and left with the others.

Bolan ordered the hoodlums to the far door. He placed a block of C-4 plastique on the poker table, set the timer-detonator for thirty seconds and escorted the hardmen down the steps into the alley. They were well away from the building when the C-4 exploded. The club's top floor rose about six inches, then sagged. There was no fire. No one would cheat gamblers at the Flamingo for a while.

Bolan told his captives, "Dump your weapons on the ground, and be glad you're still alive. Tell Carlo Nazarione he's going to be seeing a lot of me in the next week. Tell him I'll get around to him soon."

Bolan signaled a dismissal, and the three men ran down the alley toward the front of the Flamingo, where a police car had just arrived, its siren whining.

In an expensive residential district several miles away, Jo Jo Albergetti arrived home. His wheelman drove the car into the garage, then went to his own car and left. Jo Jo entered the big house via the kitchen and found his wife, Angela, sprawled on the living-room rug. She wore only panties.

She sat up and shook her ample breasts and laughed. "Hey, big guy, want some of these?" She crawled toward him.

"You're drunk," Jo Jo said, smelling the alcohol.

"So what? I'm fantastic when I'm drunk. Just took on two of your little helpers. Told them I wouldn't tell you their names so they wouldn't get shot. Oops! Not supposed to talk about guns. The two guys were marvelous! Both at once. Wanna hear?"

The phone rang. Jo Jo glared at his wife, his face revealing the anger inside. The phone rang again. He grabbed it.

"Yeah?" He listened a minute. "No shit?" He listened again. "Yeah, right... Bastard! Get Nino down there right away to start putting things back together. I want that place ready for business tomorrow night. We can't afford to have the Flamingo dark. Get moving!"

He shook his head and hung up. He scowled at his wife. "Get some coffee and then go to bed. I'll deal with you in the morning."

Jo Jo went to the garage, stepped into the Cadillac and drove downtown to check on the damage at the Flamingo.

At the Flamingo half an hour later, Nino Tattaglia frowned. He had expected Bolan would hit them somewhere, but not like this. The Flamingo was the flagship of the Nazarione gambling operation. The old man had stuck to gambling as his main source of income, leaving narcotics to the other families.

Nino talked with the cops, identified the two slain men and began looking for some solid proof. He had talked to Mack Bolan a week earlier, and the Executioner had said he would be coming to Baltimore soon. Nino was surprised at how soon. Against a wall, he found a black-and-dull-silver army marksman's badge, the Executioner's trademark. He showed it to the police.

Little was left of the gambling room. One wall had been blown into the hallway. The roof sagged. The furnishings were a jumble of twisted metal and scorched upholstery. The remains of the poker table were visible as matchstick-size splinters all over the room.

Nino marveled that Bolan had bluffed his way into the inner sanctum of the back room. He was good.

Jo Jo arrived, looked at the wreckage, swore for five minutes, told Nino to get it fixed, then left. Carlo Nazarione arrived as the police were leaving; he stayed in his car and asked Nino for a complete report.

"Looks like those two rooms upstairs will be closed for a month. A team of carpenters is coming in tomorrow morning at eight. I suppose the city engineers will want to see if the building is structurally damaged. That could mean big problems."

"Goddammit! How did the bastard get in there? Who we got on the doors? Talk to them. If they took cash to let him in, you fry their butts good. Make it so they never work for us or the other families again."

He shook his head. "Damn Bolan. First time he's hit us. Why is he concentrating on us, Nino?"

"I don't know, Carlo. Maybe you're getting famous or running such an efficient operation here that he heard of you."

"Yeah, yeah, that must be it. Flattery—I guess that's it." He frowned. "Hell, you have the place fixed up fast. We need the income. Pick a new floor man carefully—no more dummies—and move somebody up as a hardman inside."

"You can count on me, Carlo."

Nino stepped back. Nazarione powered up the window of his crew wagon and the Caddy lumbered down the street.

As Nino turned toward the club half a block away, someone tapped him on the shoulder.

"Nino!"

Tattaglia jumped. He would know that voice anywhere. He turned and saw Mack Bolan standing in the darkened doorway of a closed jewelry store.

"We got your calling card."

"That's just the start. The old man riled?"

"Yep, and this is my end of the business. I've got to get back in there and twist tails, but I need to talk to you."

They moved away from the commotion of people and police cars around the nightclub.

"I've been cooperating with Leo Turrin, but this is different. What the hell am I supposed to do if I'm in a joint and you come in spraying lead?"

"Duck!" the Executioner said. "That's why we talk, so I know where you are and how to get in touch with you. If I'm going to blast some spot, I get you out first."

"Good, I can buy that." Nino pounded a fist into his palm. "Damn! I don't know how I ever got into this. Here I am now with the cops looking for me on one end, and I got to be careful what I say and do so my own people don't find out I'm a traitor to them. You know what they would do to me?"

"I don't think you had much choice, Nino. Cooperate or face the electric chair."

"Damn, I know it. The Feds nailed me good, and Leo turned me around. Now just how much hell you going to raise in my town?"

"Depends on what's here. Right now I'm just trying to get Nazarione's attention. The word on the wire is that something big is going down in Baltimore. I want to know what it is."

Nino frowned. "Damn, I don't know what the gossips are talking about. Biggest thing I know of right now is that I'm paying two thousand a week to a crooked cop. I'd like to get rid of that bastard. He's Capt. Harley Davis, a real rogue flatfoot who's getting rich. He's the head of the burglary detail, which also handles gambling."

"And you're in charge of all Carlo's gambling operations?"

"Right. I work through Jo Jo Albergetti. He's a kind of vice president of sales and revenues. Leo figured I could work in from this end and get the fewest people hurt and still be in the middle of things."

"Why don't you just burn this Captain Davis?"

"A damn good reason. He says he has enough hard evidence on Carlo, me and half of his lieutenants to put us all away for life. If he shows up dead—for any reason—all his evidence is turned over to the cops within twenty-four hours. The Baltimore police, the D.A. and the mayor would mow us down."

"Has he got the goods?"

"Probably. At least enough to bluff the rest. So we pay him off."

"I'll get around to him. Now pay up to Uncle Sam. Find out what's making the criminal underworld so excited. Something big is happening or is about to happen in Baltimore. I want some information tomorrow. Ask Carlo. Tell him you heard about it on the grapevine and want the straight goods."

"I might be able to—Carlo likes me. Anything else?"

"Give me the addresses of four more of Carlo's gambling clubs."

"You gonna hit them?"

"Wait and see."

"Man, I'll be busy tomorrow."

Nino produced a small notebook from his jacket pocket and wrote down four sets of names and addresses. He tore the page from the book and gave it to the Executioner.

"Give me a phone number where I can reach you or leave messages. Two of them would be better. No matter what name I leave, I'm your cousin from San Francisco."

The informer gave Bolan two numbers: his home and his office in a downtown catering firm that Carlo owned and Nino supposedly ran.

"I better return to the scene of the crime. The cops must be done by now. We got to be back in operation by 6:00 P.M. today."

They did not say goodbye. Tattaglia turned back and Bolan simply walked on.

The Executioner continued another block to his rented car, and drove to one of the gambling clubs on the list. He put a full magazine in the handle of the Beretta 93-R and left the round in the chamber. From a soft zippered bag on the seat he took an army smoke bomb and slipped it into his pocket.

The Club Jasmine was half bar, half dance floor. A small combo was rocking. Bolan didn't try to find the gambling rooms. He worked toward the back, drink in hand. He sat at a vacant table and pulled the small smoke bomb from his pocket. Under the table he removed the safety pin and rolled the device. As he stood he heard the pop, then shouting as the smoke poured out.

It would sting the eyes and the lungs but do no damage. He calmly left by the front door with the first wave of shouting, frightened people and was half a block away when the fire alarms sounded.

That night two more clubs were hit by the harmless yet irritating smoke bombs; Bolan arrived at the fourth near closing time. The clientele was sparse. Before he could send the smoke grenade rolling, a waitress appeared at his table. The pretty young thing looked at Bolan, turned pale and shivered. She seemed scared.

"Can I get you something?" she asked, trying to smile.

Bolan shook his head. "No thanks. I'm about ready to go."

"You just came in." Without waiting for a reaction she sat down across from him at the table.

"Hey, I've got a small problem."

"Somebody giving you a bad time?"

"How...?" She nodded. "Yes. A real jerk. I told him he can't take me home, and I don't want to go anywhere else. I even threatened to report him to the management. He just laughed and said he *was* the management."

"When do you close?"

"Fifteen minutes. Then it takes about ten minutes to clean up." She sighed. "I know this must sound phony, but I'm not trying to pick you up. You have a kind, understanding face, that's all."

She looked at him. Bolan remained silent.

"If you could wait for me just outside and tell this jerk to buzz off, I would appreciate it."

"What's your name?"

"I'm Elizabeth Hanover. Beth. And I feel much better already! I must start moving, before I get fired." She hurried away.

When the lights blinked and closing time was announced, Bolan wandered outside. She said she would leave by the front door. A couple and a man, evidently alone, also waited. More patrons left, among them a girl Bolan recognized as a waitress. She hugged the couple waiting for her and they left.

Five minutes later Beth Hanover walked through the door. Her short blond hair was hidden under a little hat, and a scarf covered the lower part of her face. The lone man approached her and said something.

"No!" she said sharply.

Bolan hurried over and looked at the man who had touched Beth's shoulder.

"She said no," Bolan said softly.

The man snarled and swung. His fist grazed Bolan's side. The Executioner solidly punched the shorter man's midsection and then bounced a right off the side of his head.

The unwelcome suitor dropped to his knees. Then his right hand dug inside his jacket and came out with firepower.

When the gun appeared, Bolan's kick sent it skidding along the pavement. The smaller man screamed.

The Executioner slammed his hand into the man's throat softly, so as not to kill him. The guy went down with a cry of defeat and humiliation. The fight left him, and he sat on the sidewalk dazed.

Bolan crouched beside him, grabbed his left arm and smashed it across his knee, breaking the forearm like a dry twig.

The screech of pain sounded like a siren. A black Cadillac raced to the curb and skidded to a stop, and two men rushed to the fallen man. They helped him up, cradled his arm and put him into the big car, which raced away.

Beth had huddled by the front door. Now she came over, her eyes wide.

"I didn't mean you should hurt him."

"He pulled a gun. He might have killed us both."

"Oh! I never thought of..."

"Do you have a car?"

"Yes, just down the block."

They walked that way.

"Do you have any idea who that man was?" Bolan asked.

Beth shook her head. Her little cap had twisted to one side and her short blond hair showed.

"No. I've seen him at the club before, but he never bothered me."

"And he said he was part of the management?"

"Yes. I thought he was joking."

"Probably not."

Her car was in the back of the lot. She stopped by the door.

"I better follow you home in case those men are waiting for you nearby."

"I don't think you need to. His arm looked broken to me. They'll be at a hospital or doctor's office somewhere." Her eyes were suddenly angry. "You broke his arm! How could you?"

"Beth, that man was part of the Baltimore Mafia. You know what that means?"

Beth Hanover nodded and all at once she was shivering. She reached out and Bolan put his arms around her.

"Do you have somewhere else you could stay tonight? They could get your address and . . ."

"No. I'll be fine. They wouldn't dare hurt me, not now that you can identify them. I'll be just fine."

2

Mack Bolan unlocked Beth Hanover's car and handed her the keys.

"You've got it right? First you follow me. I want to be sure those goons didn't leave someone to tail us. Then when I'm sure no one else is back there, I'll blink my lights and pull over and you take the lead and drive to your place. I'll come behind you."

Beth smiled and he saw the fright fading from her eyes. She could be no more than twenty-one, slender and attractive. Bolan jogged to his car, got in and drove back to the lot. She started the engine, turned on the lights and pulled into the street after him.

He made a series of turns and reversals and one U-turn; no cars seemed to be following. Ten minutes later she led him to her place and parked in a reserved spot in the apartment-complex lot.

She met him on the street where he was stopped.

She bit her nails and looked at him. Then she remembered and pulled her hand away. "I know it sounds a little strange, but when you said they might get my address out of the records...." She shook her head and turned away.

"Beth, he really scared you, didn't he? I don't blame you. If it would be all right I'd like to sit outside your door for a while. I don't think he'll try anything, but with scum like him, you just can't tell.''

"Oh, no! You don't have to stay outside!" she said, suddenly aware he knew exactly what she was thinking. "It's just that . . ." She sighed and touched his shoulder. "If you're going to come and be my bodyguard for a while, at least I should know your name.''

"I'm Mack Scott," he said, giving her an alias that he had used before.

"Hi, Mack," she said, smiling brightly and extending her hand. They shook. "Now, that we're officially friends, I can make you a cup of coffee.''

Bolan smiled, locked his rental and they went up to her apartment. It was a small studio apartment on the second floor—one big room with a kitchenette, a bathroom and a let-down bed. The place was neat and clean. "I go to school during the day and work nights to get my bills paid. I came here from Iowa to go to school. Don't ask me why I chose the University of Baltimore. Maybe so I could get out of Iowa. I'd lived there all my life. Am I talking too much? I do when I get nervous.''

When the coffee was ready she found some grocery-store doughnuts that were two days old but still good. She said she was an only child and she was taking a course in television journalism, hoping to get into newscasting. She hoped the doughnut was okay. After ten minutes she ran out of small talk, excused herself and went to the bathroom. When she returned he saw that she had been crying.

She sat across the small coffee table from him, her eyes bright.

"So what kind of work are you in?"

"Insurance. I have clients all around the country."

The phone rang.

She looked at him, fear radiating from her eyes.

He held up his hand, let it ring five times, then picked it up.

"Yeah, what the hell you want?"

The only sound from the wire was a gentle click.

"Wrong number," Bolan said, and hung up. He watched her. "You feeling better?"

She nodded.

"Isn't there someone you can call and go visit for a couple of days?"

"I've only been in town three weeks. I don't know anyone here that well."

"How about a motel? For you alone? Look, I'm the one who caused part of the problem. Let me pay for two nights at a hotel for you. I'd feel better."

She shook her head. "No, I promised myself I wasn't going to run away from anything else. A guy wanted to marry me in Iowa. He was a 'fine catch,' my parents said. I liked him, but everything was so *dull!* So I ran away from him and my folks. But now I'm through with running."

Bolan checked his watch. It was slightly after 3:00 A.M. The goons should have been here by now if they were coming. He stood up. "Keep your door locked and bolted. If anyone knocks, dial the police emergency number. Promise?"

She nodded.

"I better go. Let me have your phone number so I can call you tomorrow and make sure you're all right." He memorized the number on the phone.

At the door she crooked her finger at him, hugged him, then kissed him softly on the cheek.

"Thank you very much, Mack. I don't know what I'd have done without you tonight. Please call tomorrow about noon. I come home for lunch." She smiled, tired but still animated. "Maybe...maybe the next time you come calling, I'll be better company."

Bolan smiled. "Lock the door." He stepped into the hall and waited until he heard the bolt slide in place. He went downstairs and moved his car so he could watch her second-floor apartment and the closest steps leading up to it. He did not need any sleep for a few more hours.

By four-thirty there had been no problems. The lights in her room had gone out five minutes after he left, and nothing else stirred in the complex. He fired up his car's engine and crept away from the curb and down the street. He had to remember to call her at noon the next day.

BOLAN SLEPT UNTIL TEN A.M., then quickly showered and dressed. He snapped on the TV set to catch the news.

"...and said he would have no comment. Here at home, police have identified the victim of an early-morning murder that on-the-scene people describe as a torture killing. Elizabeth Hanover, a student at the University of Baltimore, was found dead in her apartment this morning by a friend. The coroner said she had been gang-raped and tortured. There are no suspects in the crime and no apparent motive. One resident reported a car leaving the front of the apartment about four-thirty this morning.''

Bolan turned off the set and stared out the window. Either they had come quietly while he was in the car, or they had arrived after he left. He slammed his hand against the wall and swore.

Another innocent victim dead because of him! Someone who merely brushed against him for a few hours! If he had done it differently. . . .

He hurried from the hotel and walked for two miles, working off some of his fury. Then he stopped at a phone and called the business number Nino had left for him.

"Cousin Harley—same old voice," Nino said on the phone. "Figured I'd hear from you."

"Nino, anybody in your family get a broken arm last night?"

Nino laughed. "Yeah, I figured you'd know about that. A little enforcer named Wally 'The Beast' Franconi. A damn tough cookie."

"Not tough enough when I find him. Where does he hang out?"

"Franconi runs a poolroom over on Grand."

"Thanks, Nino," Bolan said, and hung up, figuring how to deal with Franconi. This had to be a day The Beast would remember for the rest of his life—no matter how few hours he had left to live, or how unpleasant they would be.

CAPT. HARLEY DAVIS SWORE at the phone, then picked it up. "Davis here."

"What the hell is going on down there, Davis? You know who this is. A perfectly legitimate nightclub gets blasted to rubble. Where the hell is our police protection?"

"Hey, easy. I've been having some problems. My force is spread thin. No way all the cops in the world can stop something like that. The attacker always has the advantage—you know that. We're doing what we can to find the bomber and take care of him."

"We're doing the same thing, Davis. I'm pissed at you and the department. Hell, we pay taxes. What good does it do? Now three more places have closed because some nut set off smoke bombs in them. No big damage but a lot of sick people and mad ones."

"He's trying to scare you."

"Who?"

"Hell, you know. Mack Bolan, the guy who calls himself the Executioner. He's always after...places like yours."

"So find him and nail his hide to the closest flagpole."

"I'd like to. He's made my damn ulcer kick up again."

"Fuck your ulcer. I'm losing money."

"We had to take two of your boys in on gambling charges. No way we could avoid it. I'll set it up so they can get released on their own recognizance."

"Damn well better."

"Send me anything you have on this Bolan. Isn't there a picture of him? I'll check the wires on him. FBI had something going a while back."

"You get something going. You shut this joker down, and do it damn quick!"

"Yeah. Nothing I would like better."

They hung up. Captain Davis slouched in his chair in the glass-enclosed office. At least the glass went to the ceiling to provide a little privacy, soundwise. He was forty-nine years old and awaiting his thirty-year retirement, due in three years. Before then his plan was to have a nest egg to keep him on easy street. Hell, he might have to stay on a few years more, if he could keep raking in a hundred thousand a year from his friends.

He laughed softly. Friends, yes, just as long as they knew that he had enough on them to send them to prison for life. He had and they knew it. It became a delicate matter of compromise and cooperation.

Now this damn Executioner guy storms into town. Not even he could get in the way of the timetable. Davis took off his shoe and rubbed his foot. It still hurt once in a while. He'd been in too many fights with drunks and dopers to get off without any injuries. Even been shot twice. Damn, the years had gone fast!

He brushed back what was left of his brown hair and pushed his reading glasses in his pocket. Still had perfect distance vision—that was what counted now.

Bolan the Bastard, Jo Jo used to call him. Yeah. He'd have someone check the BPD files, then call the FBI.

In the meantime he could have a bigger problem. He consulted his phone list, then called a number he seldom used, almost never from this office. The call went to the Alonzo Fruit Company. When an operator answered, his message was brief.

"I'd like to talk to the man. This is Keno." He hung up and returned to work on a burglary case that two of his detectives had almost wrapped up.

His phone rang and he picked it up. "Yeah, Davis here." When the other voice came on he sat up straight and smoothed down his hair.

"Yes, sir, good to talk to you, too. Sir, this Mack Bolan matter. Is this going to hurt our timetable?"

The voice on the other end was slow, relaxed, with a touch of Old World Italian.

"We don't think it will affect us. We know about this small problem and our people are working on it. We will solve it perhaps today, and then nothing will be in our way. This Bolan is human—he bleeds. If you bleed you can die."

"Yes, sir. I'm doing what I can here. He's a lawbreaker and we'll exert the full power of the police in tracking him down."

"Good. Now one small insect is left in your garden. We would be happy if it could be taken care of as quickly as possible."

Sweat beaded on Davis's forehead. He wiped it with his hand. The phone showed wet spots.

"Yes, sir. That matter will be taken care of... today."

"Good. I knew we could count on you."

"Thank you for returning my call, sir."

"Yes. And remember, be sure it's done today."

The wire went dead and Captain Davis hung up slowly. Damn! He had to do it today. He shook his head, breathed deeply, then dialed one of his plain-clothes men. The cop came in at once.

The two men in business suits huddled; two hundred dollars changed hands well below the glass line in the wall, and the cop left at once.

Captain Davis finished his coffee and made another call. "Need to see you for a minute, Paulson," he said.

It was arranged.

Ten minutes later the captain's assistant drove him down Johnson Street. They had set up an undercover burglary sting operation involving cops acting as fences to buy stolen goods; the transactions were videotaped. They were approaching the operation when the police radio in their unmarked unit came on.

"This is seventy-three Baker. I have a suspected robbery in progress in the 3400 block of Market Street. The big warehouse. Request a backup."

Captain Davis grabbed the mike. "This is X-twenty-seven. I'll take that backup by seventy-three Baker. We're within two blocks of the location."

Lieutenant Paulson hit the siren and swung into the next lane.

"No siren! We don't want them to know we're coming!"

Lieutenant Paulson shut it off, leaving the red light blinking. Paulson had spent five of his twenty-six years on the force. He was a go-getter and an absolutely honest cop. He wasn't the captain's choice as his second in command on burglary and gambling for nothing. Paulson was Mr. America, easygoing, fearless, bright and ambitious. He had earned his B.A. degree in three years, studying nights and weekends.

"We'll check the sting later," Davis said, his adrenaline pumping. He checked the service revolver in his snap-on belt holster. His .38 was there and ready. In his back pocket he felt his cold piece.

The unmarked police car stopped near the warehouse. A cruiser was nearby. The two cops in it grinned when they saw Davis. He nodded at them. They had each earned an envelope with fifty dollars in it.

"Captain, we saw some dude start out of the warehouse with a sack over his shoulder," the first uniformed cop told him. "The guy saw us and ran back inside like a jackrabbit."

"Right, Officer. You cover this door. Send your partner around to that side entrance down there. Paulson and I will go in and rout him out."

They jumped on the nearest loading dock, and slid into shadows.

"We'll work straight down the main aisle," Captain Davis said. It was a general storage warehouse. "You check to the left, I'll keep to the right."

They worked slowly forward with their revolvers out. They were halfway when Davis motioned Paulson to follow him into the aisle on the right. No direct overhead light shone on the narrow alley between the tall stacks of boxes containing television sets.

"You watch at this corner," Davis whispered to Paulson. "I heard something over there." As Paulson looked around the boxes, Davis took from his pocket a .38 with the serial numbers filed off. He backed up six feet and shot Paulson in the temple.

He died instantly.

Davis drew his own service revolver and fired four times into the ceiling.

"Down here!" Davis screamed. "Down here! I think Paulson is hit!"

Davis wiped his prints off the cold gun with his handkerchief, then slid it thirty feet down the aisle. He mopped sweat off his forehead, ran three more aisles over, then saw a uniformed cop coming.

"Hold your fire! He got out a far window down there, all the way on the end."

The uniformed officer found Lieutenant Paulson first, as Captain Davis had planned.

"Christ! The lieutenant is dead!" the cop said as he knelt beside the body. "Jesus! You never said—"

"Don't just sit there!" Captain Davis roared. "Call for an ambulance! Move it!"

The cop ran down the main aisle, the fifty dollars in his pocket feeling like blood money. He'd had no idea anyone was going to die! He radioed for an ambulance and the coroner. He tried to throw up, but he could not.

An hour later people still milled around the death scene. An assistant chief, Larry Jansen, kept shaking his head. Paulson had been the chief's fair-haired boy. Jansen had helped promote him over a dozen older men who had scored higher on the testing.

Davis watched the two cops warily, but they said exactly what they were supposed to. The suspect fled into the warehouse. They didn't see that he was armed. They blocked off all the escape routes but one. The killer used it after shooting the officer. They had no idea why he dropped his gun. Perhaps the captain had wounded him, maybe hit his arm and the weapon fell. It was too dark in the warehouse to describe the man except by saying he appeared to be black and in his twenties.

Captain Davis sat on a box. He was visibly shaken. He did not have to fake it. He had killed before, but never a cop he had worked with, and not this way. He knew he had to do it, but he was sure he could never do it again. He had paid his damn dues! If the Mafia don wanted more from him, he would have to raise the pay scale to three thousand a week.

Chief Jansen touched the captain's shoulder.

"Harley, take the rest of the day off. Don't come in tomorrow, either. I know how this hurts. You'll get over it. It'll pass. But don't rush it. Come on, I'll drive you to your car."

3

After he talked with Nino Tattaglia, Mack Bolan looked up the pool hall on Grand, then dialed. He talked to two flunkies before he got Wally "The Beast" Franconi on the line.

"Is this Wally Franconi?"

"Yeah. Who's asking?"

"Recent acquaintance of yours. Remember the guy who broke your arm last night?"

Bolan waited until Franconi stopped screaming. Eventually, the flood of words and insults tapered off. When the Executioner could interrupt, he spoke sharply.

"Franconi, you're not very well adjusted. Are you still there?"

"I'm here, you fucking bastard!"

"Good. We should get together. I figure I proved to you that you need a guy like me around."

"Hell, no! I . . . hey . . . whaddaya mean?"

"Protection. Those goons who were with you didn't help you much. You ain't all that big without your rod, and like I thought, you sure as hell need some help."

"Man, I gotta say you got guts. But even if I agree to a meet, why wouldn't I show up with six guys bigger than you and bust both your goddamned arms?"

"You're smart, that's why. And so am I. Busting me up ain't gonna make you no money. Staying alive and healthy so you can use your equipment makes you a money man. I can help you stay in action and turning the coin. Just figures."

"I got protection. Who you with before?"

"West Coast. Got a little hot out there. Boss said take off a year. I don't need the money. But I work for six hundred a week."

"Hell, I don't know. Maybe we should have a meet and talk. No promises."

"Hey, none needed. I'm nuts about racing. Know that little one-eighth-mile dirt track just north of town by Parkville?"

"I can find it."

"Just to talk. About noon."

"I don't know. Damn arm still hurts."

"Take some pain pills. A long drive in the country'll do you good."

"Okay, okay. I'll be there. Just be sure you come alone."

"Right, Franconi, alone. See you then."

It was eleven o'clock when Bolan arrived at the little race course. There was a dirt track. There were rickety stands for about two hundred people and pits with no garages. A summer operation. The gate to the track was open, so he put the rented Chevy around the oval at a leisurely pace, figuring to shake loose somebody in charge.

A grease-marked man wearing only shorts and running shoes waved the car into the pits. The Executioner stopped.

"You run the show here?"

"Me and the bank."

"Hear you got some hot destruction derbies going."

"Now and then."

"You got a car I can buy for the destruct?"

"Might. Cash?"

"Right on the radiator. It's got to have a good solid rear end and reverse and low forward."

"Any make?"

"Most of them are several makes."

The man laughed. Bolan figured he was thirty. The Executioner got out of the car and extended his hand. "Scott's the handle. Where is this bucket of bolts?"

The man said his name was Castile and that he owned the spread. He led Bolan to a battered car and outlined its history.

The destruct racer had started life as a '69 Chevy, had outlived three engines and six radiators and all its fenders, but it still owned both low and second and reverse.

"Got a V-8 in there right now that can snarl your pants off. I won the last two destruct derbies we had here with that little cranker."

"How much?"

"Well, I got six seventy-five in her and she's a winner. Purse goes two hundred. Eight-fifty and she's yours."

"Sold, if I can use your track this afternoon for a couple of hours. You'll have to clear out. Want the

place all to myself and this guy who challenged me.''
The Executioner took out his wallet and counted out
nine one-hundred-dollar bills. ''Close enough,'' he
said.

''You own it,'' Castile said.

Bolan found what he needed in the shop after Castile left. He put strands of strong wire in six places
around the front bumper, and looped them for quick
use. Then he wedged some sheet steel between the
steering wheel and the dash—a perfect shield, in case
he was fired upon. The pliers went in his back pocket.

He fired up the Chevy and backed it around the
track. A giant X-shaped roadway marked the infield,
where the close-clearance races were held. He soon got
the knack of driving in reverse, putting the battered
hulk exactly where he wanted it.

It was eleven-thirty by the time Bolan was ready. He
put two weapons in the battered veteran—the ''flesh-
shredding'' .44 AutoMag and a French infantry rifle,
the 5.56 FA MAS, which is easy to handle, has great
balance and keeps on target even when firing fully
automatic. It spits out 3-round bursts or full-auto and
holds a 25-round magazine. Four loaded mags were on
the seat beside him.

The Executioner counted on Franconi bringing at
least two cars full of armed soldiers. He figured The
Beast would talk first, size him up and plan some dia-
bolical end to the man who had humiliated him before his peers.

Satisfied with the weapons and the battered Chevy,
Bolan drove to the small shack that served as office,
ticket booth and living quarters for the·owner. He

nosed the vehicle into the shop section backward so he could race it into combat. He climbed the open steps to the upper floor and opened the window to check his field of fire. Perfect. The enemy crew wagons would probably not stop until they were directly below.

His only problem was getting Franconi alone inside the shack. The upstairs window would be a good firing point to fall back on. He checked the Chevy destruction monster and removed the weapons. If he stood at the front door, he should be able to lure Franconi inside. He knew the Mafia hit man would not be satisfied with a quick kill. And he would not let any of his men do the killing except in an emergency. This would be Franconi's show, and that would be his fatal mistake.

Bolan waited at the front door. At five to twelve, two black crew wagons rumbled off the side road, then swung into the dirt lane toward the shack.

The Executioner wore no weapon. Big Thunder lay on one side of the door and on the other the French chatter-gun was hanging on a nail.

He wiped his hands on a rag as the Mafia rigs came to a halt twenty feet from the door.

A six-foot-six-inch-tall goon got out of one car and walked with apelike strides to the shack. He was big, ugly and mean looking.

"Boss wants to see you," the Cro-Magnon said, jerking his thumb toward the car.

"Soldier, you tell Wally I don't like the inside of wagons with twenty guns in my nose. Have him come over here and you guys stand guard."

The goon stared in surprise. Usually people did exactly as he suggested. He shook his head and returned to the car. The door was still open. He said something, then repeated it, and Wally Franconi, scowling, slid out of the back seat. His left arm was in a cast to the elbow.

Franconi took a deep breath and stepped within three steps of Bolan.

"Okay, wise-ass, we talk. Who the hell are you? Where you from? What can you do?"

"Name is Mike Scott, from L.A. I'm a wheelman, bodyguard, persuader and action man."

"And you use your feet—I remember that!"

"Yeah. I'm ready to show you how I can wheel. Want to look at the inside of this place? Got my destruct derby car in here and it's a beaut."

Franconi's face lit up. "Mean where those assholes back up and try to kill off all the other cars? Last one running wins?"

"That's the contest. She's mostly Chevy. Got her nosed in here. Want a look?"

"Always wondered how they beefed up those things. Always wanted to try it."

"Hell, try mine. Come on in." Bolan stood to one side. Franconi made up his mind, gave a hand signal and walked into the shack.

When Franconi stepped out of sight of the crew wagons, the Executioner slammed the big silver .44 AutoMag down on his head. Bolan dragged the unconscious body to the front of the destruction derby car, hoisted it to the front bumper and, using the positioned wires, tied it securely lengthwise along the bumper. Bolan put boards under the wires before cinching them up so the wire would not cut into flesh. When the mobster was solidly fastened to the bumper, Bolan grabbed both weapons, put them in the car and fired up the V-8. It popped and snarled, and then he roared from the shack in reverse, turning so the hoodlums could plainly see their boss.

Leaning out the window, he fired one AutoMag flesh-shredder into each crew wagon, then raced to the far end of the dirt oval and waited. One of the crew wagons moved slowly along the edge of the track.

Bolan put the rig into low and ground forward toward the nearest crew wagon, with the Beast leading the way on the front bumper.

He could imagine the confusion and shock in the crew wagon as the men tried to figure out what to do. At last someone decided the destruction derby rig must not hit the crew wagon and raced it away. Bolan fired three rounds from the French army rifle and watched the Cadillac soak up the bullets. He wondered how far they penetrated. One shattered the rear window, turning the safety glass into ten thousand small granules.

Bolan chased them halfway down the track, then stopped and punched ten rounds into the front tires. Two or three found their mark, the right front tire blew and the rig slowed to a stop. Handguns came out the windows, popping at him. Then all was quiet. The goons were afraid they would hit the boss on the bumper.

Slowly Bolan accelerated in reverse. He could hear someone screaming. It was Franconi.

Bolan ignored the sound and raced the engine. He barreled across the track toward the stricken crew wagon. Its driver gunned it away, flopping tire and all, to the cover of the other Caddy.

Bolan kept coming. Franconi kept screaming. The Cadillacs parted as the Chevy rushed toward them, and as soon as it had passed a dozen shots slammed into it. Bolan ducked and spun the wheel, turning and driving forward straight for the hoodlums. One man dived from the car and into a two-handed stance with his weapon. The Executioner cut him down with six rounds from the FA MAS. The second crew wagon turned toward the road. The remaining rounds in the MAS magazine shattered its right rear tire. When the rubber blew, the car stopped.

Bolan slammed a fresh magazine into the FA MAS and fired. As the windows shattered, the Mafia soldiers fell out the far doors. Two tried to run for the highway, but they were brought down.

Three down. How many to go?

The Executioner raced past the closest Caddy, ducked, slammed into reverse and rammed the luxury car, sending forth from its radiator a cloud of steam and a stream of water into the dirt.

A dozen shots from handguns peppered the demolition car. Bolan turned it around and raced toward the crew wagon again. He stopped just in front and, aiming over the metal shield, blasted the remaining windows of the second Cadillac. Two men slid out on the far side and Bolan wished he had some grenades. He circled, firing at anyone who moved.

He aimed the AutoMag at the gas tank. Three heavy rounds pumped into the volatile fluid before it exploded, showering human parts and pieces of metal over the track. One lone Mafia hoodlum staggered away from the pyre. The Executioner slammed a flesh-shredder through him.

Bolan crawled over the immovable door of his Chevy and looked at Franconi, still wired to the front bumper. His eyes were wild, his mouth slobbering drool. He had been screaming as loud as he could, but now his voice had given out and only a croak came through. Bolan slapped his face until the hoodlum's eyes focused.

"This is for Beth Hanover."

The Executioner got back in the Chevy, raced the engine and stormed after the last crew wagon.

He saw a white handkerchief flutter.

Bolan killed the Chevy's screaming engine fifty feet from the dead Cadillac.

"We give up!" a voice shouted.

"You wanted Franconi, you got him!" someone else said.

Bolan fired three rounds from the French army rifle into the windowless Caddy.

"You give up the way you let Beth Hanover give up when you raped and tortured her last night?"

"Franconi did it!" came a third voice.

Three of them. He wanted one to get back to Nazarione and tell the Mafia boss exactly what happened at the little track and how two crews and his best hit man were wasted.

"Okay, you have one chance. The three of you run for it. Get out the far side and run for the road. One of you will make it. That's better odds than you gave Beth."

The three jumped from the car and raced for the road. They spread out and ran as hard as they could.

Bolan nailed the first with a 3-round burst. The second took nine shots to put down. He fired over the head of the third, who made good his escape.

When Bolan was satisfied both Mafia goons in the dirt were dead and that only he and Franconi were left alive, he checked the cars.

He backed up the destruction derby Chevy, then raced toward the flaming Cadillac. At the last second Franconi screamed and he wound the wheel to the right, grazing the crew wagon. Four times he flashed past the furiously burning Caddy. Then he stopped and checked on his reluctant passenger.

Franconi had passed out again. Bolan made sure the wires were tight, then slapped Franconi awake. The hit man screamed and groaned.

"It's all over, Franconi. I just passed sentence. For what you did to Beth, you don't deserve to live. Nothing elaborate, just a little car crash." Bolan started the Chevy, and pushed it into first. "Have a nice ride, pal."

He put a rock on the accelerator pedal, aimed the screaming Chevy at the burning Cadillac fifty feet away, tied down the steering wheel and released the parking brake.

The destruction derby car raced forward, picking up speed. Franconi helplessly traveled more than thirty miles an hour toward the Cadillac. When they hit, the Chevy's gas tank exploded, gas and gas vapor gushed over the Cadillac and both cars burned with a furious intensity, incinerating everything in sight, even melting some of the metals.

Bolan turned and walked away, the FA MAS on his shoulder, Big Thunder in his hand.

"It isn't much, Beth," the Executioner said. "But I hope it settles the score. Maybe now you can rest in peace."

4

As the Executioner drove away from the racetrack on a country road, a fire truck charged toward him, its siren wailing and red lights flashing. He pulled to one side to let it pass. He figured the fire at the track had attracted them. But he was too far away to be connected with it.

He had about half an hour to get to Herring Run Park, just off Sinclair, where he was to meet Nino Tattaglia.

His forehead wrinkled as he reviewed his mission in Baltimore. He had to find out what deadly, destructive event was about to go down here, and hoped Nino would be able to tell him.

The Executioner was a big man, more than six feet tall and a finely muscled two hundred pounds. Right now his cold blue eyes were trained on the road. He was not moved one way or the other by the dead men he left behind. Eradicating human evil had long been a necessary fact of life for him.

This was an everlasting war, and it had brought him to Baltimore. It was a war he knew no one man could win.

Bolan was a realist. He knew that one day he would move too slowly, or a bullet or grenade would be in exactly the right spot and the warrior would be killed. But until that happened, he was charging ahead, he was digging into every dirty Mafia operation he could find, he was pumping the Mafia full of hot lead. He was also living large and making every second count.

He would make the Mafia fear him for as long as his strength and life remained.

The holy war against the Mafia had become Bolan's purpose in life.

And so, to fight again.

He swung the rented Chevy into the park, watching for a man on a picnic bench. He saw him and parked.

Nino slid into the car and frowned. "Bad for my image to be seen sitting on a park bench."

"What's going down in Baltimore?"

Nino's eyes widened. "You'll never believe it. It's a capo's dream!"

"Try me."

"The Nazarione family's about to take over the whole goddamned police department! The operation has been in place for months and is coming down to the last phase. Already we've got two city councilmen pinned down and two of the four assistant chiefs!"

"Blackmail?" Bolan asked, his face turning grim.

"Most likely, or exposure on some corruption. The family has the whole damn department on the hook, not just a hundred officers and some captains! The whole town will become our playground!"

"What two assistant chiefs have been caught?"

"I don't know. Hell, I was lucky to get this much. But it's all on a timetable, so much done each week, and we're near the end of the game."

"You and I are going to call off the game because of a number of deaths in the Nazarione family, Nino."

"Maybe. You hear about the cop getting killed this morning?"

Bolan shook his head.

"Some lieutenant in a shoot-out with a robber. And guess who was on hand, 'working' with the lieutenant? Our own Capt. Harley Davis. Which probably means the lieutenant was honest and they gunned him down because he couldn't be bought or bribed or blackmailed. Odds are that Captain Davis pulled the trigger with three or four bribed cops as backup."

"What's the next target?"

"That much I do know," Nino said. "It will be Assistant Chief Larry Jansen. And it's set to go down in two hours. I'm supposed to be along for extra protection."

"I'll be there as soon as it happens. When you see me, hit the deck and stay down. I may have to use quick target selection."

"Don't worry about me. Just be sure you make it. This is a key man in their plans because he's next in line to be chief."

AN HOUR LATER, Nino Tattaglia helped carry Assistant Chief Jansen from a car at a back unit of a motel. The door was open and they put the chief on the motel bed beside a black girl. The lady was nude and dead, and her body and the bed were covered with blood. There were six long slashes on her torso. Three stab wounds marred the soft dark skin.

Polaroid pictures were taken of the chief in several positions beside the girl. In one, his hand was taped around a bloody knife and the blade pushed into the dead girl's chest. Enough of his face was showing to be recognizable.

"Strip him!" Big Jake Milano said. "Get his pants and shorts off and spread him out over her." Milano was satisfied. He was getting good at this. Third time! Hell, he'd get a bonus. This time he'd take the old lady on a cruise of the Caribbean.

"Got enough pictures?" Big Jake asked.

"One more," Tony Larasso said. He put another print on the dresser.

Suddenly the door exploded inward. Before anyone could move, a figure dressed in black stormed in, waving an Uzi submachine gun. Big Jake went for his side arm, caught three slugs in his chest and collapsed against the far wall, dead.

Mack Bolan sized up the four others in the motel room at a glance. There was a kid with a camera to the left, and two hardcases behind the bed to the right. Nino stood near the back.

"Don't move!" Bolan barked. One of the hardcases dug for his belt holster and the Uzi spit out five rounds, nailing him against the wall for a few seconds until his corpse slid slowly to the floor.

"Anyone else?" Bolan asked. The kid dropped the camera, leaned over and vomited. Bolan pointed at Nino.

"Take out your piece and drop it on the bed, then get this other goon's gun and put them both under the bed. Check out the puker here for hardware."

Nino did as he was told. He turned, holding his hands high.

"Get the chief's pants on fast!" Bolan snapped.

As Nino complied Bolan grabbed the developed Polaroid prints from the dresser and pushed them inside his black jersey. He picked up the camera and ripped out the film, then checked out the door. No problems.

Bolan pointed to the kid and the older man behind the bed. "Both of you, strip off all your clothes, then lie down on the bed beside the girl. Move it!"

Both men shed every piece of clothing and lay down gingerly on the bloody bedspread.

Nino put the chief's pants and shirt on him. The cop was starting to come out of his drugged state.

"You, carry that man outside," Bolan barked at Nino. "You make any noise, or one false move, bad-ass, and I'll blow your head off." Nino picked up the blood-smeared cop and took him to the door.

Bolan's rented Chevy sat six feet away from the motel room. The two Mafia lookouts were hunched over beside the door as though they were sleeping. Nino knew they would never wake up. He lowered the chief into the passenger seat and closed the door.

Bolan waved Nino back inside the room and followed him.

"Now, tough guy. Off with your clothes, too. Then join the others on the bed."

Bolan grabbed the bundle of clothing, closed the door, stepped into the Chevy and drove to the front of the motel. He stopped to call the police from a phone booth, watching the motel-room door as he dialed. As soon as he had them on the line, Nino stepped out of the motel room and ran full tilt down the alley.

The Executioner told the police a girl had been killed in the motel by Mafia hoodlums. He gave the address, hung up and deposited the garments at the side of the booth. Then he drove off. Half a mile away he pulled over to the curb. Slowly Bolan brought the groggy cop back to his senses.

Chief Jansen shook his head, his vision fuzzy, his mouth tasting foul.

"What the hell?" He rubbed his eyes, trying to clear them. He looked at Bolan. "Who are you?"

"A friend, Chief Jansen. Just relax—you're safe now."

"Safe? Where are we?"

"In my car on the street. I just pulled you out of a motel."

"Motel? I went out for a cup of coffee with one of my sergeants. He said he owed me a store-bought cup and he had a problem he wanted to talk about privately."

"And then he slipped you some knockout drops. Look at the blood on your hands and your clothes."

"Oh, Christ! Mine? Where did it come from?"

Bolan made sure the chief was totally back in the current time zone, then explained the whole thing to him.

"Damn! I fell for it. Now I don't know who to trust! We've got to get some units over to that motel!" he exclaimed, still a cop.

"I reported it. The place should be swarming with cops by now."

The chief nodded. "You didn't tell me why somebody tried to get blackmail evidence on me in that motel. Are you sure the girl was dead?"

Bolan took out the pictures. One of them had blood splatters on the back.

The policeman's eyes widened in astonishment. "They were setting me up. What for?"

"Certain groups in town want to take over the police department. They have already blackmailed two assistant chiefs. You were the next target. That officer who was shot this morning was probably murdered by one or more of his fellow officers."

"No! Captain Davis was with him. One of our best men."

"Are you sure? Check out Davis's bank account. He's taking two thousand a week in payoff money from the Mafia."

Chief Jansen stared at his bloody hands.

"You're sure of this?"

"Yeah. You won't have to dig far into Davis to find out he's as dirty as hell."

The chief opened the ashtray on the car and burned the pictures of himself. He saved the other shots of the body and nodded at Bolan.

"I still don't know who you are, but it looks like I owe my whole career to you. Another ten minutes and they would have had me so tightly tied up I never would have gotten out. How do you fit into this?"

"Just trying to be helpful." Bolan turned on the car radio to an all-news station and kept the sound low.

"Where can I drop you off, chief?"

"Take me to the side door of the downtown station. I have some clothes there."

Bolan heard something and turned up the volume on the radio.

"And Baltimore police said it was one of the most grisly killings they have seen in a long time. The body of the woman lay faceup on the bed. The bedspread was soaked with blood, and the nude bodies of two men, both shot, lay sprawled on the bed. Two more men, sitting against the steps outside the room, had also been shot dead. Police have blocked off the area and are talking to all witnesses.

"One man in the motel room next door said he saw one young man running naked down the alley about ten minutes before police arrived. A car that had been parked in front of the room was seen leaving the area, but no one could say who was in the car, or what the license number had been.

"In other news..."

Bolan shut it off.

"You didn't say anything about the four dead men."

"Right, I didn't. Let's leave it at that. When you identify them you'll find them all to be Mafia soldiers connected to Carlo Nazarione, who claims he has no organized-crime affiliations."

"At least we know better than that." The cop shrugged. "Hell, I won't push to find out who you are. I'll never be able to thank you for what you did for me today. Now, one ride downtown, then I want to get showered and dressed and back out to that motel."

As Bolan let the chief off fifteen minutes later, the cop stared at him a moment. "Have we met somewhere before? Something about your face seems familiar."

"Thanks. I used to do some modeling—a lot of those rugged outdoor-type print ads. I did a lot for one cigarette company."

The chief nodded. "Yeah, that was probably it." But as the car swung away and the cop hurried through the private entrance into the police department's top-brass area, he knew he had not seen the man's face in an ad. It was on a Wanted poster. And the guy wore the same black suit. It would come back to him. Damn, he wished he could remember.

He went down the short hall to the chiefs' men's room with its lockers and showers. He undressed before anyone else came in, stuffed the bloody clothes into a plastic bag and then showered off the blood. He had never seen so much blood in a shower before. Wrong. That bathtub suicide when the drain plugged.

Half an hour later the chief was dressed and heading for the motel in the passenger side of an unmarked car. When he and his driver arrived he took command of the investigation. As he pushed through the crowd behind the police tape he remembered who the man was who had saved him—Mack Bolan, the Executioner, the one who was at war with the Mafia and wanted by the FBI and in dozens of states!

5

After Mack Bolan dropped off Assistant Chief Jansen, he stopped at a phone booth that had a directory in it and found the address of a small printing firm. He located one close by but passed it up when he saw a one-man operation down the street.

Inside, the place had the musty, slightly alkaline odor of paper stock mixed with the acid tang of the printer's inks.

A short, bald, middle-aged man with half glasses came from behind a rotary press that was hissing with every turn.

"Morning!" he said, smiling. "What can I do for you today?"

"I need a business card. On the front I want a name and a phone number, and on the back the nearest thing we can find that resembles a five-dollar gold piece."

"Easy. And you need it in five minutes."

"No, that's the easy part. I don't want it for two hours."

"Should be a snap. Cost you as much as five hundred of them would."

"I'll give you fifty dollars."

"Good, that's what five hundred costs."

Bolan wrote out the name and the number, and the little man pawed through one box after another. He turned, holding a piece of plastic that had something engraved on it.

"Found something I can use. I'll set the type and burn a plate and we should be in business."

"Brown ink on the front and gold ink on the back, right?"

"Cost you another thirteen dollars for cleanup on the press, if you want a good job."

Bolan gave him a fifty-dollar bill and a twenty, and said he would be back.

His next stop was a phone booth, where he consulted a list of numbers that Nino had given him. He found the Baltimore godfather's number at the top of the list. He had to go through three men before he got the Baltimore capo on the phone. Bolan had heard Augie Bonestra from Brooklyn testify on TV a few months back. Now he imitated his voice.

"Yeah, this is Augie up in Boston. Hear you got Bolan down there."

"Right, Augie."

"I sent a man down early this morning. Want him to watch how you handle the Bolan thing, case he ever comes my way. Guy's name Lonnie Giardello. Can handle himself. Sent him down and then forgot to call. Should be there in an hour or two. Let him see what's going on, Carlo."

"Sure, Augie, no problem. I hope he brought a card."

"He's got one of mine. Good talking, Carlo. I got to get moving."

They said goodbye and Bolan hung up. He grinned. He was not sure how close Augie and Carlo were, but there had been no hesitation about accepting the voice as genuine.

Now for the rest of his outfit.

Bolan went back to his small hotel and changed clothes. He wore a brown pin-striped suit, a red tie and a brown snap-brim hat that he'd bought in a men's store. He looked like your average hoodlum soldier. Or maybe a little conservative. He could pass.

Back at the print shop the old man was blow-drying the ink with a hair dryer. He showed Bolan three cards. The Executioner picked out one and cut the other two up into strips with a small paper cutter and put them in his pocket. He thanked the printer and left. In his car, he signed the card boldly: Augie Bonestra.

There was no problem finding the fortified mansion where the boss of Baltimore lived. Bolan brought from the hotel a small bag packed with a few clothes to hide six charges of C-4 plastique with radio timer-detonators. He caught a cab to the big house, headquarters of the Mafia empire in Baltimore.

The cab stopped at the massive iron gate. A soldier ambled out and looked inside.

''Giardello?'' he asked.

''Yeah, from Brooklyn. How did you know I was comin'?''

''Hey, this is Baltimore. We know everything. Crawl out and pay off the hack. It ain't a far walk from here.''

The guard pointed Bolan to the side entrance and said someone would meet him there. A small man with sharp features and a sniffling nose opened the door, showed him to a bedroom and said Don Nazarione would like to see him when he was settled.

Bolan grinned, playing the part.

"Hell, how about now?" He adjusted a .45 automatic in his shoulder leather and walked behind the small man along the hall. The mansion was what he expected—overdecorated, plush, expensive, ostentatious.

They went up a small elevator to a huge office forty feet long on the third floor. On that level there was a putting green—a golf-green carpet with four holes and miniature flags. Across the green sat Carlo Nazarione behind a large, old-fashioned cherrywood desk with massive carved feet. An IBM computer sat on the edge of the desk with a daisy-wheel printer beside it.

The don was not what Bolan expected. He stood six-four, had the classic Italian dark good looks, a full head of black wavy hair and was not more than forty years old.

"So you're the hotshot from Augie?"

"Yes, sir."

The capo came from behind the desk and Bolan walked up to him, went down on one knee and kissed the offered ring. He stood and stepped back, waiting as he knew he should for Nazarione to lead the conversation.

"Did Augie send me anything?"

"Oh, yes, sir!" Bolan reached in his pocket and took out the card. He handed it to the Mafia chief who looked at it casually and pushed it into his pocket.

"You've done some research into this problem?"

"Yes, sir. I'm the Boston expert on the bastard."

"Good. You can tag along. You want something special, talk to Vinny here." He pointed to the thin-faced man who had met Bolan at the door. "Outside of that, don't get in the way, and if we get a Bolan alert, you'll go along. You got a piece?"

Bolan opened his jacket, showing the butt of the .45.

"Yeah. We got some better hardware. Have Vinny show it to you." The godfather nodded. The interview was over.

For the next half hour Vinny piloted "Lonnie Giardello" around the layout. He introduced Lonnie to everyone and left him with a six-man crew on alert in the basement recreation room. A door led to a driveway where a crew wagon waited, ready to roll.

"We're on alert for Bolan," one of the soldiers said. "That asshole surfaces anywhere in town, we get a call and we're rolling in two minutes."

"I'd like to come along," Bolan said.

The soldier shrugged. "If Don Carlo says show you, we show you."

"Good, I'll be around. Don Carlo told me to get acquainted with the layout. What's outside?"

"Six-car garage, tennis court, swimming pool and lots of lawn."

Bolan nodded and wandered outdoors. In the garage he looked over the cars—two Cadillacs and one

Lincoln. From his pocket he slipped out two packages of C-4 and pasted one under the front fender well on each of the two Caddy crew wagons. The detonators were set for channel one on his radio-controlled signal box.

He walked around, went back inside, found the kitchen and bummed a roast-beef sandwich and coffee, pleading that he had not eaten on the plane.

The Executioner met Nino Tattaglia in the hall and the turned-around hoodlum's mouth dropped open in surprise.

Bolan came up quickly. "Hi, I'm Lonnie Giardello. Just down from Boston to watch the Bolan fight."

"Yeah. I'm Nino Tattaglia," he said, his face still showing surprise.

"Didn't I used to know some of your people in Brooklyn? Bunch of Tattaglias up there. There was a Joe and Frank, as I remember. Any of your people?"

"Not that I know of. Need a guide around this place?"

"I could use one."

They talked quietly then.

"What the fuck are you doing? Half the town is looking for you and you charge in here!"

"I was invited. Best way. I see you got away from that motel room before the cops arrived."

"Yeah, barely. Somebody saw me. At least nobody in the family suspects me. Thanks for that."

"Who killed the girl?"

"Big Jake, the guy you wasted first. He enjoyed it, the bastard!"

"Any way I can look in the weapons room? You have one here?"

"Sure. No one man runs it. Usually it's locked. Let's go check it out."

It was in the basement next to the recreation room. Several of the pool players looked up and waved when Nino came in. He talked to a couple of them for a minute.

"The weapons room open? Wanted to show our loaner around."

The men laughed, and the one Bolan had talked to first unlocked it. "We got in a special order this morning," he said. "Look at these beauties!"

Spaced out on a workbench on clean wipe towels lay three Uzi submachine guns.

"Damn!" Bolan said. "They full-auto?"

"As full as you can get. They forgot to send us any ammo, but it should be here tomorrow."

Bolan picked up one of the stubby little submachine guns that had been developed by the Israelis from the Czech models 23 and 25 chatter-guns years ago. It was still one of the most effective in the world.

He slipped out the 32-round magazine that would hold the 9 mm parabellums and whistled.

"What we could do with these in Boston!"

"Get your own," Nino said.

The other Mafia soldier laughed and returned to the pool game. It was his shot.

Bolan picked up a tool off the bench and went to work on one of the Uzis. In two minutes he had stripped off enough parts so he could remove the firing pin. He reassembled it and did the same thing to the next one. Just as he finished that one, two more soldiers came in to look at the new weapons.

As they fawned over the Israeli burp guns, Bolan planted another cube of C-4 plastique under a case of ammunition. This one had been set for detonation by a transmission on the second radio channel. The triggering device in Bolan's suitcase looked like a radio the size of a pack of cigarettes.

Nino and Bolan eased out of the room, watched the pool game and then wandered outside.

"You are crazy!" Nino said. "The first time they try to shoot those weapons they'll find out they have no firing pins."

"Let's hope it isn't too soon. Right now I need you to show me three more vital spots where I can hide these little surprise packages of C-4."

"Plastic explosives? Just be sure to tell me before you light the damn fuses."

They put the other three plastic bombs in hidden places around the mansion. The last one went in a small niche in the wall opposite Nazarione's office.

They walked outside in the soft Maryland evening.

A horn bellowed on the ground.

"Bolan alert!" Nino explained. "Let's go!"

They ran for the crew wagon near the basement door. Bolan got in the first car and Nino the second. When they were filled, the big Cadillacs roared out the driveway, barely waiting for the gate to completely open before racing through.

"Where is he?" Bolan asked the Mafia soldier wedged in the back seat next to him.

"Damned if I know," he said.

The driver explained that some big dark guy supposed to be Bolan was busting up a gambling spot uptown.

When they got there, the ruckus was still going on. Two of them covered the rear door and five others, including Bolan, stormed into the club and spotted the troublemaker. He held a chair in one hand and a butcher knife in the other. The five converged on him; he swung the chair at Bolan.

The Executioner grabbed the chair, jerked it forward, throwing the man off balance. As he flailed his arms and dropped the knife to regain his balance, one of the Mafia soldiers slammed into him with a shoulder block that carried him to the wall. They grabbed his arms, twisted them behind him and marched him out the back door.

The man was about twenty, blond and blue-eyed.

He gave his name and it checked with the ID he carried.

"Can't be our man," one of the hoods said. "Too young, too blond—no way."

Ten minutes later the Caddy was heading back toward the Nazarione mansion. The man at the club had been enraged at losing his week's pay on the gaming tables and tried to even the score by breaking up the place. The on-site security swore up and down the guy was Bolan and they were not going near him without shooting first.

"Hell, he was no more the Executioner than I am," said one of the soldiers beside Bolan.

"Yeah, or me," Bolan said.

The goon looked at him and laughed. "You look about as much like his picture as that dude we left in the alley back there with his arms broke."

Bolan had not been able to stop the "penalty" the young man underwent for smashing up two tables in the club. He could have stopped it, but it would have blown his cover.

One man swung up an Uzi submachine gun. He shook his head. "Damn, I wish to hell that ammo had arrived. I'd have greased his ass good with thirty rounds and never let up on the trigger."

Bolan watched the man caress the gun. The odds were two to one its firing pin had been removed. The Executioner still did not like the odds. He would get to the third Uzi if he could before he bailed out of the place.

He had learned part of what he wanted to know about the enemy camp. They were "up" for this battle with Mack Bolan. They had some good equipment, and some of the men were sharper than he had seen before in the average Mafia goon squads.

When they got back to the mansion, there was a general meeting of fifteen soldiers and one lieutenant as they talked about the operation that afternoon when Chief Jansen got away.

"How did he get the two guards outside?" the lieutenant asked.

"Shot them, the radio said," one of the hoods volunteered.

A man named Frank was the leader of the discussion. Now he looked around.

"The whole idea is to learn from that mistake. If you're put on guard, do it! Your life depends on it. If we got a job going down and you're out there, the guys inside depend on you. So make damn sure nothing and nobody gets at you or past you. With this Bolan bastard, you don't ever get a second chance. Just ask Big Jake or Tony L. Their funerals will be day after tomorrow. Only the families of the men are to attend."

That quieted them for a moment. Frank saw the mood.

"All right. So next time we get him, and then all of you can go to *his* funeral!"

They cheered, Bolan with them, then they quieted.

"You might wonder about another try for Assistant Chief Jansen who we missed today. Don Nazarione just decided we blow him away. It's all we can do now. Okay, that's all for tonight. You guys will be getting more briefings. We think the more you know about what we're doing, the better you can help get it done."

Bolan got next to Frank as they walked out of the recreation room. He had been introduced before.

"Frank, I got to make a phone call. Augie said contact him tonight sometime. He said be careful about the line. What'd he mean by that?"

"You're reporting back to Augie Bonestra in Boston, right? I'll check, but I'm damn sure what he meant was not to call from any phone inside this place. The cops have a way of putting two and two together. Wait a minute—I'll check with somebody."

Bolan went up to the first floor with Nino and waited around the TV set until Frank came back.

"Yeah, Lonnie, I was right. Call Augie, but do it from a pay phone down at the shopping center. It's a mile straight down the road. Harder to trace calls from a pay booth."

"Wheels?"

Frank went outside with Bolan and whistled up a crew wagon. The driver bailed out, and Bolan thanked him and drove to the front gate. It opened automatically. Frank had called the gate guard telling him to let the next car through.

Bolan grinned as he wheeled down the road. He knew there was no way he could have sneaked out of Don Carlo's armed fortress without somebody getting suspicious. He also knew that Nazarione would not want a long-distance call from his house to another Mafia family don. They had to let him go outside to make the call.

At the shopping center Bolan parked and walked across half a block of parked cars to a phone booth. He called the Baltimore police department and left a message for Chief Jansen. He told them, "I have a tip that Carlo Nazarione is going to try to shoot down Chief Jansen in the next twenty-four hours. Tell him to lie low for two or three days." Bolan hung up before they could trace the call. Even if they had the automatic readout of the calling number on their system, the Executioner would be miles away before any radio-dispatched police unit could arrive at the pay phone.

He wasted another half hour, then rolled back toward the big house that Mafia money had built.

The Executioner pulled up to the entrance. The heavy iron gate stood open. Unusual. He drove ahead, saw no one in the guardhouse. More lights were on now in the drive and in front of the big house than before, when he had driven away. Trouble. Bolan put the rig in gear, angled the car down the middle of the drive, kicked the lights up to bright, then hunched low and jumped out and sprinted fifteen feet into the shrubbery at the side of the drive.

In the darkness, he ran for the gate. It was a trap. He turned and saw the car swerve toward one side of the drive, but it recovered and rolled slowly into the lighted section in front of the house.

Twenty shots barked into the quiet evening, then a dozen followed, and soon more gunfire ripped and punctured the heavy car, blasting out all the glass, killing the engine, blowing out the tires. Somebody wanted to be sure that the driver wound up with his head in a bucket.

Mack Bolan sprinted out the front gate, which was still unmanned, and ran down the winding roadway toward the first lights at the corner a block away. Just as he turned into the next street, he heard tires squealing at the gate. The Executioner ran into the dark driveway of the second house and stepped behind the attached garage.

He touched his .45. It was still in place and loaded. Evidently the godfather had sensed something wrong and called Augie Bonestra in Boston. It would not take them long to discover the hoax and set up a trap of their own.

Bolan saw a crew wagon wheel along the street, moving slowly, with men staring out rolled-down windows.

Maybe next time, the Executioner thought. There was no chance they were going to find him tonight. It might take him a little longer to get back downtown, but he would catch a taxi sooner or later.

As it turned out, it was later.

6

The men of the Baltimore Police Department swore you could set your watch by the movements of Chief of Police Stephen C. Smith. He arrived at his second-floor office at 0749 every morning. He went over the status reports on his desk from the past two watch captains, made any recommendations at once and cleared his desk.

By 0802 he had greeted his front-office staff and had poured a cup of coffee from the communal pot, then started the rounds of his assistant chiefs, looking for any problems they might be having. He had delegated more work assignments than any former chief had ever done. It was working well.

This morning he was up as usual at 0600. His driver called for him at his suburban home at 0720 and he had twenty-five minutes to read the *New York Times* on his ride to work.

The chief's sedan had just rounded the first corner heading toward the boulevard and eventually the expressway when another car jolted away from the curb and roared toward it.

Patrolman Donald Connors saw the car through his rearview mirror.

"Something's happening, Chief!" Connors shouted. "Car back there coming up fast. Get down, Chief! Guns are showing out the windows!"

The chief glanced around, saw the long gun aimed at his car and dived to the floor of the back seat.

The black Cadillac behind them raced forward, a shotgun boomed and thirteen double O buck lead slugs slammed with thundering force into the chief's sedan. They tore through the side windows, blew out the windshield, dug into the heavy side panels of the rear door.

Three of the slugs tore into Patrolman Connors just over the starched shirt collar of his uniform. He slumped over the wheel, dead. The horn was blaring. His foot lifted only slightly from the throttle. The car jumped the curb, knocked down a pair of small trees and rolled across a lawn until it crashed to a stop against the wall of a two-car garage.

Before the Mafia crew wagon could stop, another car raced up behind it and the driver lobbed a contact grenade over the roof so it landed on the black Cadillac's hood and exploded.

Jagged shards of steel drove through the windshield and decapitated the driver. The second man in the front seat caught burning shrapnel in both eyes.

The driver's foot lifted from the pedal and the Cadillac ground to a halt. The explosion had blown apart the ignition system under the hood.

Before the surprised hoodlums in the back seat could leave the car, a second grenade ripped open the gasoline tank. The gasoline ignited in a whooshing roar, creating a spectacular funeral pyre for the Mafia killers inside the car.

The man who had thrown the grenades pulled his rented Chevrolet to the curb, leaped out and ran to the chief's wrecked car.

Chief Smith crawled out the rear door. Bolan helped him, then urged him toward the Chevrolet.

"There are men in that burning car!"

"Not men—Mafia scum," Mack Bolan said. "And there probably is a backup car. We've got to get out of here fast!"

"Who are you?"

"It doesn't matter. Is your driver dead?"

"Yes."

By then they were at the Chevy. Half a block behind them a car spun away from the curb.

"Here they come!" Bolan shouted. He leaped in the passenger side and slid over as the chief jumped in beside him. Then Bolan had the sedan moving. He ground around the first corner he came to, tires screaming. When the Executioner looked behind him, the black Caddy crew wagon was gaining.

"What's the quickest way out of town?" Bolan asked.

The chief looked behind, then at the grim expression on his rescuer's face.

The chief told him the turns to make, scowled as Bolan ran two red lights and two stop signs. When they were away from the heavily populated suburbs and on a country road with only a few houses scattered along it, Bolan said, "Look in that suitcase in the back seat. Get out that Uzi submachine gun. You have your service revolver?"

"Yes," the chief said. He got on his knees in the seat and reached into the back. "Hey! Everything in this suitcase is illegal!"

"Be glad of it, Chief Smith. If we're lucky and you can use some of those weapons, we might be able to get out of this alive. Can you use that Uzi?"

"I've fired them before. In Korea we didn't have anything quite this fancy."

Bolan flashed him a grin. "You'll do."

The Caddy had been at a disadvantage on the quick turns in town, but on the straight road the big engine made the difference as it came closer and closer. Bolan speeded up, found the spot he wanted on the sparsely traveled country road, then yelled.

"Brace yourself, I'm doing a slide stop. We'll be sideways in the road, and we both go out your door. Stay low, take the Uzi and some extra magazines and be ready to defend yourself. These Mafia hit men don't care how they kill you."

Chief Smith nodded. He grabbed the Uzi, three extra magazines and two frag grenades.

The Chevy screamed into the braking slide and stopped, almost fully blocking the narrow road. The Caddy could pass if it slowed and took it easy on the shoulder, but Bolan did not think the Mafia driver would try.

They left the car by the passenger door. Bolan opened the rear door and pulled the suitcase to the edge of the back seat for easy access.

"Here they come," Bolan said. "Let's give them a welcome."

"They have to shoot first," the chief said.

"They just killed your driver!"

"That was a different car, different men."

The Caddy slid to a stop thirty yards away. Four pistol shots ripped into the morning air. Two of them caught body metal, two more went through the front windshield.

Bolan lifted the French army rifle and shattered the crew wagon's side windows with six rounds.

Bolan's next burst went between the Caddy's wheels. When the firing stopped he heard a scream of rage.

"Get behind the front wheel and stay low," Bolan said.

An answering burst of fire came under the Chevy. He heard one automatic weapon. It had to be an Uzi.

A man sprinted from the Cadillac, angling toward a row of trees and brush at the side of the road.

The chief lifted the Uzi and sent three rounds at him. He missed. He corrected and the next five rounds put the runner down.

Bolan watched as the Mafia soldiers tried to lay down a protective hail of fire. The windows in the Chevy broke into thousands of granules of glass. Bolan scattered two more bursts from the rifle, then reached in the suitcase for a fragger.

"You've used these?" he shouted to the chief over the sporadic pistol fire.

The chief nodded.

"Good. Let's do it. You put one at the front of the car, and I'll get one to the rear." They both pulled the safety pins and looked at each other. Bolan bobbed his head. The chief threw first. His grenade hit short and rolled within three feet of the Caddy before it exploded. Before the noise died down Bolan threw his small bomb slightly behind the rig so it would roll just beyond it. The explosion came first, then the screams of pain as jagged steel met flesh.

An Uzi opened up on full-auto, screaming twenty 9 mm parabellums into and under the Chevy. Bolan threw one more grenade and rolled it under the Caddy, hoping it would explode just on the far side.

When it went off there was silence on the country road for a moment. A car came up behind them, and the chief waved it back, flashing his badge at the surprised driver. The car turned and raced away.

The silence continued from the Mafia machine.

"I'll go check it out," the chief said.

"No, Chief. You didn't even make the SWAT squad. I do this kind of work all the time. You keep that Uzi handy."

Without a wasted motion, Bolan jumped into the six-foot ditch at the side of the road. He had taken no enemy fire. He bent over and ran along the ditch, two fraggers swinging on his black combat harness. Big Thunder jolted where it was tied down at his hip. He carried the French army rifle like a toy.

When he was beyond the Cadillac, he rose and looked over the lip of the ditch through some tall grass.

He saw only one man standing, and he was bleeding from the head and chest. The man turned and sent a dozen rounds from the Uzi in the ditch twenty feet away from Bolan, then dropped the weapon, let out a soft cry and collapsed.

Bolan fired two shots into the air, but without reaction from the Mafia soldiers. Slowly he moved toward the battered crew wagon. Four dead men lay on the tarmac. One other moved, wounded with shrapnel. Bolan kept the French rifle on full-auto as he ran into the scene. He checked the bodies, then looked at the man who had moved. He stared up at Bolan with angry eyes.

"Man, they didn't tell us it was gonna be a goddamned war! You must be that Executioner guy."

Bolan nodded.

"Damn!" the hoodlum said, then died.

It was over. Bolan called to the chief. The cop ran around the Cadillac and stared at the massacre.

"It looks like that hill in Korea where we lost so many guys."

"They attacked us—remember that."

"I don't even have a radio."

"Let's see if the Chevy will drive. They forgot to shoot out the tires at least. We might be able to start it."

They got in and Bolan ground the engine three times, then it started. They headed toward the nearest telephone.

Bolan told the chief about the Mafia's attempted takeover.

"They knew they couldn't turn you, so you had to be killed. That's what happened to Lieutenant Paulson yesterday. We're almost certain that Capt. Harley Davis killed him." Bolan continued laying it all out, about the try for Assistant Chief Jansen the day before and that two of his assistant chiefs already had been blackmailed.

"That's the story, Chief. I'd suggest that you lie low for a day or two. Let them think they nailed you."

Chief Smith shook his head. "It's so much to accept at one time. Captain Davis! One of my best men. He's taking two thousand a week."

"Men do strange things for money, Chief."

"But not you. You must be this Executioner we've been hearing about. Big story about you in the paper this morning. The FBI says to shoot you on sight." He chuckled. "You save my life once, and then the second time. I guess you broke some laws, but I had deputized you. You were helping a law-enforcement officer in his sworn duty. But we're in the county jurisdiction here.

"I better call the sheriff. I think I'll stay out here somewhere. Let me make that call, then run me in to the little town up ahead. It's got a motel and some cafés. I've got my credit card."

He shook his head again and got out of the car. They were parked outside a general store. "Better make that phone call." He rubbed his hand over his face. "How many...how many men did you and I kill today?"

"They weren't men—they were Mafia killers who had each murdered some Mafia enemy to get in the club. What we did was a public service. Wait until you look at the rap sheets on those guys."

The chief nodded and went into the store. He returned quickly.

"Sheriff already had a report and two cars are on the way. We better get out of here. I made it an anonymous report."

Half an hour later Bolan had driven the chief to within a block of a motel and let him off. Then the Executioner put all his weapons back in the suitcase along with his combat harness, slipped on a sport shirt and left the shot-up Chevy on the street. He took his suitcase, walked away and caught a taxi into downtown Baltimore.

Bolan changed hotels, checked in under a different alias and sat in his room considering his next move. He phoned the rental agency and told the clerk where the car could be found. He mentioned it had been somewhat wrecked and reminded the anxious clerk that the rental fee and the insurance had both been prepaid.

CAPTAIN HARLEY DAVIS of the Baltimore Police Department had taken the day off as Chief Jansen had suggested, but he did not tell his wife. Instead he drove his unmarked car to an apartment house just off Franklin Street and went up to suite 1111. Eleven was his lucky number.

A woman wearing a short nightgown came to the door. She peeked around the barrier and when she recognized him, swung open the door.

"Hey, you gonna bust me?"

"Of course not, Francie. Any friend of Carlo's is a friend of mine."

"He said you might be around. Had breakfast?"

"Yes, but I'm still hungry," he said, looking at her chest suggestively.

She stepped back and smiled. "None of that until I have breakfast. A girl has to keep up her strength."

"You eat, I'll watch," Davis said. He sat in the little kitchen observing the woman. It was a delight. She never failed to excite Davis, no matter what she wore. Right now his motor was running at high throttle.

The apartment she lived in rented for at least fifteen hundred a month. But she didn't worry about that. Carlo Nazarione picked up the rent and the tab for her clothes and everything. He was not the jealous type. He offered her around, and Francie seemed to dote on the attention and the variety.

When breakfast was over, Francie crooked her finger at him and walked to the bathroom. She found a new toothbrush for him, still in a plastic wrapper, and indicated he should brush. She brushed her teeth and washed her face, then put on her makeup as he watched.

When she'd finished she winked at him, then slid out of the nightie, handed it to him and walked away. Captain Davis growled and started after her. Francie was one of the fringe benefits of being so friendly with Don Nazarione.

The phone rang just as Davis pulled off his tie. Francie sprawled across the bed, grabbed the phone and rolled onto her back.

"Saks Fifth Avenue, lingerie and notions department." She listened. "You really need to talk to him. He's gonna be pissed right out of his pants." She paused. "Hell, it's your problem now." She tossed the hand set to Davis, who stood beside the bed unzipping his pants. He caught it and put it to his ear.

"Yeah?"

On the other end of the line a uniformed cop named Tony Ricca talked so fast Davis yelled.

"Hold it already! Damn, I can't make out a word you're saying. Take it easy and give it to me slow."

"Okay. Johnny King, the other guy in blue with me yesterday on that warehouse killing, is wetting his drawers. He's so strung out I can't get him even to report back to the station. He's weird. Keeps playing with a crucifix and mumbling.

"He says you didn't say nothing about nobody getting killed yesterday. He didn't sleep last night, and he's off his rocker. Keeps confessing that he helped set up the lieutenant. Keeps yelling our names. I don't know what to do with him."

"You in your marked patrol car?" Davis asked.

"Yeah, where I been sitting for the past hour. Dispatch is ready to ream my ass."

Davis zipped up his pants and looped the tie back around his neck.

"Tell me where you are, and don't move. I'm on my way. I can reason with King one damn way or another. Where are you?"

Captain Davis wrote the cross streets down in his little book, and put a wide knot in his tie. He bent and kissed Francie's lips as she lay on the bed.

"No playtime?" she asked.

"Postponed, Francie. Later."

"Anytime," she said and rolled over. "Business, I guess."

"You bet, Francie. Takes one hell of a lot to get me out of your bedroom this way."

She waved, and Capt. Harley Davis walked out of the apartment.

Twelve minutes later he approached the corner where Officers King and Ricca sat in the prowl car. He parked behind them beside a fireplug. He waited. Both officers got out of their car and came toward his.

"Get in back," Davis said.

They both crawled in and Davis turned, his face angry, his voice controlled with effort.

"What the hell is going on here?"

King looked up, his eyes wary, his voice unsure.

"Captain, I'm no angel. I turned the other way a couple of times when I shouldn't have. I've seen prisoners get roughed up for no cause, I've seen evidence jimmied around because I knew damn well the assholes charged were guilty. But I've never been part of any murder."

Davis's face mellowed. "Aw, shit! Is that what you think? I figured you had something important. Didn't Ricca tell you? We were walking along the aisle of the warehouse when we discovered a sneak thief. First thing I hear is this handgun blasting away.

"I get out my piece and return fire. The bastard wasn't more than three feet from us when he blew away Paulson, missed me and darted behind some boxes and ran out the back window. Hell, I thought

Ricca explained it all to you. We had a damn two-eleven going down!''

King rubbed his face with one big hand. Then he looked at Ricca. "No kidding?"

"Hey, I been trying to tell you, but you wouldn't listen to nobody, just pissing and moaning about Lieutenant Paulson."

"That's the way it happened, Ricca?" King asked, grabbing the other officer's arm.

"Damn right. I thought you heard when the captain explained it to Chief Jansen."

"Hell!"

"Yeah, you been screaming up the wrong damn pole for nothing. You better apologize to the captain for dragging him out here like this."

"Captain, what can I say?" King mumbled. "It just looked like a setup, and then when Lieutenant Paulson got shot . . ."

"King, no problem. Don't worry about it. We have to keep on top of things. And I'd appreciate if you forgot whatever you were thinking, all right?"

"Yeah, Captain, sure. I just wiped it out of my computer banks."

Captain Davis reached into his pocket and peeled three twenties from a gold money clip.

"King, this is for all your worry. Go out to dinner and dancing with the wife somewhere. Forget all about this."

The men nodded and stepped out of the car. Captain Davis looked at Ricca.

"Ricca, you have anything on that gambling operation you spotted on Thirty-fifth?"

"A little." He looked at King. "Johnny, get the rig warmed up. I'll be right there."

King got into the patrol car.

Ricca leaned in the captain's car window.

"Kill him, Ricca. Do it tonight. He's ready to break. He could take both of us down. Use a bad car wreck, hit-and-run and into the bay somewhere. Make it look good."

"I get a bonus?" Ricca asked.

"Two thousand. Now get it done!" Captain Davis scowled at the uniformed patrolman as he returned to the squad car. It would not be long before Ricca himself would have to be taught a lesson, Captain Davis decided.

7

It was early evening when Bolan finished making the phone calls. He could not find Jo Jo Albergetti at his office or any of his usual hangouts. Bolan took a chance and drove past the Albergetti home in a classy residential district. Lights were on in the downstairs windows.

He parked three houses down, got out and walked back to the house where he punched the doorbell. He heard the six-note chime inside and waited.

The woman who opened the door held a glass in one hand. She looked at him, took a sip from the glass, then opened the door wider. She was obviously drunk, and Bolan could tell that she had trouble focusing. She wore a filmy negligee that hid very little of her body.

"Hi, I'm Angela. You looking for a good time?" She pulled open the garment, and thrust a thigh forward. Bolan concentrated on her face, hoping he would be able to get some answers.

"Is Jo Jo here?"

"Not so you could notice. But you're here and I'm lonely. Why don't you come in and we'll have some laughs, get friendly." She shrugged out of the negligee, then drained the glass in one long swallow.

"You know where your husband is?"

"What does it matter?"

She smiled. She was shapely, blond and hungry for him.

Bolan stepped back.

"Do you know where Jo Jo went?"

"Yeah, some damn pool tournament at the Billiard Palace. Now come inside and let's play house."

The Executioner returned to his car, glad Angela was Jo Jo's problem, not his.

The Billiard Palace was a high-class pool hall with a sunken area for tournaments. A sign inside the door indicated that tonight a small tournament of eight ball would be played. It was an open tournament costing fifty dollars to enter, single elimination on a draw from a hat, a straight ladder tourney, winner take all— so said the sign.

Eighteen men and two women had signed up, so there was one thousand dollars in the pot. All the sharks in town would be there.

Bolan slid into a chair behind a small crowd and watched a shooter drop the four ball on the break, get a good spread and run the table. The opponent didn't get a shot. Bolan walked closer to the tournament board. Jo Jo had played and won. He would be around somewhere. Bolan had not met him but knew he was short, balding, of a ruddy complexion and always wore a red plaid cap on his head.

Jo Jo held court at the end of the bar. Three men around him were listening to his story of the game.

"Nothing to it!" he said too loudly. "Just skill and talent and you win every time."

The Executioner edged into the group.

"Like to buy the winner a drink," he said.

Jo Jo grinned, then shook his head. "Nope. Can't afford to get sloshed. Have to shoot again in about half an hour, and I got to be rock solid."

Bolan moved in closer.

"That was a great game, Jo Jo," the Executioner said.

"Damn right!"

Some of the group moved away. Bolan finally stood beside Jo Jo and grinned. "Carlo said I should look you up."

Jo Jo was suddenly wary. "Yeah? Why?"

"I'm just passing through—a driving vacation. Stopped by to pay my respects to Carlo."

The others had faded away. They spoke in low voices.

"Oh, hell, fine. Everybody's a little touchy right now, this damn Bolan character being in town."

"Heard about him. Somewhere we can talk, private? My friend on the coast wants to talk to you, if you're interested. Don Nazarione said he wouldn't stand in your way."

"A move?"

"Where can we talk?"

Jo Jo began walking toward a room that contained an ornate pool table. Around the walls were easy chairs, a wet bar, a big-screen TV and another door on the far side. After Bolan entered, Jo Jo locked the door.

"You said West Coast, right?"

"True. My don has heard lots of good things about you. He's heavy into the gambling end and wants somebody to head up that division. Be like a vice president, about eighty or ninety men working under you.''

"You're talking big bucks. A draw and a percentage?''

"You bet. My don knows how to treat his people. And then there's all those beauties on the beach to consider, too.''

"Southern California?''

Bolan grinned and drew the silenced Beretta 93-R from his shoulder leather.

"No, Jo Jo, southern hell. You're getting careless in your last few hours. I'm a friend of Elizabeth Hanover. If you say 'Who?' I'll shoot you down right now.''

"Hey, I didn't have nothing to do with that. Franconi did that on his own.''

"He's your chief enforcer.''

"Yeah, but he's on a long leash.''

"Not anymore.''

"Yeah, I heard.'' Jo Jo shivered. "They said they never found nothing of him but his teeth. What a way to go.'' He frowned. "That was you! You're Bolan the...''

"Bastard," the Executioner filled in. "You're right. Want me to roll over and play dead so you can collect that five million dollars head money?''

"Look. I didn't know nothing about that girl. I swear! Franconi's been in trouble that way before. He's wild. No way you can blame me for what he did on his own!''

Suddenly Jo Jo broke for the rack on the wall and pulled down a pool cue. He grabbed the tapered end and swung the heavy handle.

"Now you're getting smart, Jo Jo. Going up against a silenced Beretta automatic with a pool cue."

The hoodlum swung the cue viciously at Bolan's chest. The Executioner jumped out of the way and shot him in the shoulder. The Mafia lieutenant dropped the cue, momentarily held his arm, then scrambled for the cue, which Bolan's boot held to the floor. When he reached for it, the Executioner kicked Jo Jo's head, smashing him backward on the floor.

"You've been calling the shots too long, Jo Jo. You've forgotten how to roll with the punches."

Bolan put the Beretta away. He lifted the pool cue and held it in both hands.

"On your feet, scumbag."

Jo Jo shook his head to clear it as he began to struggle up. When he straightened, a wicked-looking blade materialized in his fist. He lunged at Bolan, snarling.

Bolan used the stick to parry the thrust, then feinted forward with the tapered end. Jo Jo Albergetti tried to step back, but was blocked by the billiard table.

Bolan used the opening he sought and brought the tip of the cue down with lightning speed. The wooden lance pierced the mafioso's chest, entering his heart. Bolan's two hundred pounds of might powered it forward. The Mafia lieutenant was dead within ten seconds.

Bolan left him where he fell, the cue sticking out of his chest straight into the air. He dropped a marksman's badge on Jo Jo and checked the far door. It led to a hall toward the rear of the building. A few moments later he found a back door into the alley and went out.

He was at his car before anyone noticed Jo Jo's absence.

It was nearly an hour later when a waitress went into the private room and found Jo Jo.

DON CARLO NAZARIONE sat at the big desk in his office on the third floor of his mansion and shook his head.

"How many men we lost on the Chief Smith hit? Ten? Are all of them dead?"

The other man in the room, Ardly Scimone, his second in command, stared at the godfather.

"I'm afraid so, Don Nazarione. Five shot, the others dead from hand-grenade fragments, and the fires. It has to be the Executioner again."

"He's cutting us into hash! Why can't we stop him?"

"We could call for help from the commission."

"Hell, yes, but by the time reinforcements get here we'll all be dead. How many men did we lose on that try against Jansen?"

"Four."

The tall man stood and walked around the putting green, elevated to allow for the holes with their small flags.

"Well, we missed him, but there's a chance that they got the head man, Smith."

"If that's so, then one of our men could move into the chair." Pacing, he lit a cigar and puffed.

"We've still got the resources and the men to pull off the grab. We'll continue. Keep everything on schedule. We've got the two inspectors and the two city councilmen on the payroll. They'll do what we tell them. And we have a hand-picked candidate for the new chief when we need one. Yes!" Nazarione smiled.

"So keep everything moving. We're going ahead. Ard, let me know of any problems. We have two more days. Let's hope nothing else goes wrong."

Nazarione saw Ardly out and descended in his private elevator to the "home" apartment on the second floor. This was sacred territory. No stairs led here, only the private elevator. Here Carlo Nazarione became a family man.

His wife, Sydney, smiled at him. She was his rock. Here he was totally away from business. None of the hardmen ever came here. They were not allowed. Only personal servants—and just three of them—were admitted. It was essential to him to keep his family and business separated.

Tall and blond, Sydney was not the good Italian girl he was supposed to marry. But she had been good for him, good to him and never thought about another man. Their two children, fourteen and sixteen, were away at school.

"Hard day?" she asked.

"Seems they've all been hard lately. But I want to forget that. What are we doing tonight?"

"A movie, the one everyone's been talking about— I got a video cassette of it. We can see it right here."

Carlo laughed. "You know just how to pick me up when I'm down. I hope it'll always be this way."

"It will. Soon the kids will be grown and gone and you and I will be old and gray and we'll sit on the beach in Acapulco or maybe Greece."

He kissed her forehead and led her to a soft chair in the living room where an enormous TV screen covered one wall. He adored Sydney but did not share her faith in the future. He lived in such an intense world, with so many pressures. The police and the government were easy to battle. Now he was suddenly faced with an enemy who thought the way the family did and who fought with intense savagery without holding to the strict ethics of the police.

Carlo tried to throw off the black mood. Then he thought about all his men who had died in the past two days and a tremor darted up his spine.

No! It could not be. He would not let it happen. He had let the Executioner invade his headquarters once with that fake story about his friend Augie Bonestra. That would not happen again. They had Mack Bolan right there! They should have killed him a dozen times, yet he had escaped, laughing at them, and knowing a lot more about them. Carlo would never let anything like that happen again. Security was of the utmost importance.

Carlo prayed that it was not too late, that he had not made a fatal blunder, one that could not be corrected.

8

That evening at nine-thirty, Assistant Chief Gene Vincent finished work, signed out at the front desk and went to his car. Lately he had been working overtime on a secret report on gambling in Baltimore and how it had touched even some police officers. There still was a lot of work to do, but he was making progress

Vincent entered the official car and locked it. His mind was still on his report. Yes, he was right in presuming that the more money offered, the more takers you would find in any kind of a bribery situation. Just what it took to push a normally honest cop into going on the take, he was not sure. If he were lucky, he might find out.

He left the parking lot and headed for the expressway. As usual during the forty-five-minute drive home, he would relax totally.

He turned right and took his usual shortcut along a side street toward the highway's access ramp. He saw a car coming up fast behind but decided it had time to slow down.

It did not slow down.

The other car rammed the chief's rig, slamming it across the curb and into a pole. The seat belt held, but

Chief Vincent swung forward and hit the steering wheel with his chest and the windshield with his head. It was not enough to make him lose consciousness. His first thought was that he would be terribly late getting home.

The car stopped, and someone ran to it, banged on the door, then smashed the window to unlock it.

Vaguely he saw a face over him, then felt something wet splashed over his face and suit. It smelled strange—whiskey! He was being soaked with booze! He tried to call out, but his mind was still foggy from the knock on the head.

He was being held in place. He heard the car keys come out of the ignition, the trunk opening and closing, the keys shoved back in the ignition.

For an instant his vision cleared and he saw two men staring at him, and then a .45 automatic moving toward him. The blow on his temple didn't seem hard, but the whole scene suddenly became too difficult for him. He saw the darkness closing in and then he relaxed and let it come and fell into a drifting, uneasy unconsciousness.

Something sharp, painful stung his nose. Chief Vincent turned away but the smell followed, stringent, biting, strong. He moved his head once more but the smell again followed. Vaguely he recognized the odor as smelling salts.

"I think he's starting to come out of it," a voice said from a long way off.

"Chief! Chief Vincent!" The voice was closer this time and he blinked and saw lights.

Pain darted through him as his eyes opened.

Assistant Chief Gene Vincent knew he was alive.

"What..."

Then he heard a soothing and familiar voice.

"Take it easy, Chief. You don't seem hurt bad. Knock on the head where you hit the windshield. Don't see how you didn't get battered up more since you didn't have your seat belt on."

Chief Vincent blinked again, and stared at the fuzzy shapes and forms. He shook his head and the pain knifed through him again.

He blinked and his vision cleared. Leaning into the car over him was Capt. Harley Davis, the gambling specialist.

"Davis," Chief Vincent said. "What happened? Somebody rear-ended me?"

"Chief. We got it all under control. You sure did get a jolt in the backside, but whoever it was tore out of here. A patrol car has already sent in a report. We got cops all over the place, so just relax."

"Head...hurts like hell."

"Yeah, lacerations. Doesn't seem too bad. Can you move? Try your arms."

He moved his arms, then his legs.

"Get me out of here, Davis."

"Yes, sir. We've got an ambulance on the way."

Slowly they pulled him from the small space between the seat and the steering wheel. The wheel had not collapsed or crushed, Vincent noticed. Wasn't it supposed to?

He swung his legs to the sidewalk and remained seated.

"Chief, you smell like a roadhouse. We found an open bottle of bourbon on the floor. You taking a little shot on the way home?"

"No, I haven't had a drop. Give me a breath test right now."

"No need for that, Chief," Davis said. "Just wondered." He reached in and took the keys from the ignition. "We need to check the trunk to be sure there aren't any internal fuel-line or gas-tank leaks. That rear end got jolted pretty good. Hope we can get the trunk lid up."

Sirens wailed and more police cars arrived. When Vincent looked up the next time he saw Larry Jansen watching him.

"Hey, Gene, relax. It doesn't look all that bad." He glanced away. "What?" he called to someone.

Captain Davis came to his side.

"Chief, I think you better come and look at this."

The two officers went to the rear of the car. Davis pulled back an old blanket in the trunk to reveal a plastic-wrapped bundle. Chief Jansen bent in and inspected it.

"Is that what it looks like?" he asked Captain Davis.

"I'm not sure, sir. I was just checking for a gas leak. I thought you better look it over."

Jansen lifted the wrapped bundle. Beneath several layers of clear plastic, a white powder was clearly visible.

"Look at that marker on the side," Davis said. "It's a recording number from our narcotics vault where we keep the impounded evidence."

"I see it, Davis. That's the forty thousand dollars' worth of cocaine we took three days ago. What's it doing in the chief's trunk?"

"Sir, I think we better ask Chief Vincent that," Davis said. "We have half a dozen officers who saw me open the trunk just as you drove up."

Jansen closed his eyes. Davis had set up Vincent, then suckered Jansen to give the final shot to end Vincent's career. No matter what happened in the investigation, Vincent was finished as a law officer. Davis had taken out another top management officer who would not be blackmailed.

Captain Davis cleared his throat. "Sir, do you want me to handle this, since you are such close . . ."

"Yes, Captain, take Vincent downtown and book him."

"Yes, sir."

"First let me have a word with him." Jansen went around the car. He looked at Chief Vincent and shook his head.

"Gene, there's a package of cocaine in your trunk. It's been stolen from the department's drug storage lockup. Did you know it was there?"

"Cocaine? Hell, no. And I remember somebody pouring whiskey all over me just after the wreck and somebody smashed the window to unlock the door, then reached in and took the keys out of the ignition. . . ."

"Remember that, Gene. Right now, we've got to book you. We'll get it all straightened out. We've got some criminals wearing uniforms right now. We'll get them all blasted loose. Hang in there with us, and remember what you just told me."

He stepped back and motioned to Captain Davis, then got in his car and drove with elaborate caution toward the police station. He did not want to be in any "accident," as Gene Vincent had been. No matter what would eventually transpire, Gene was probably finished with the department, unless they could prove a lot of things quickly. Damn!

Half an hour later Assistant Chief Jansen was back at headquarters. Chief Smith had not been to work all day. No one knew where he was. That in itself was unusual.

By midnight, Smith still had not come in. A phone call came through to Jansen's desk. It was the first time the phone had rung.

"Yes?"

"Chief Jansen?"

"Uh-huh."

"This is the guy who pulled you out of that bloody situation yesterday."

"Yes, again my thanks. They just wiped out another assistant chief. Planted some cocaine in his car."

"They also tried to kill Chief Smith this morning. I think we need to talk, somewhere safe. I'm allergic to police stations. Can you walk north on Greenmount just north of Thirty-third? I'll be along to pick you up. No escort, no visitors—just us two."

"Of course. After what you did for me, there's no chance that I'd double-cross you."

"Good. I'll see you in fifteen minutes."

Sixteen minutes later Mack Bolan pulled a rented Buick to the curb and blinked the lights. A tall man in a suit approached, looked through the car window and got in.

"All hell is breaking loose. Vincent is in jail, our other two honorable assistant chiefs are being blackmailed and now you say Chief Smith is in hiding? They actually tried to kill him?"

"You must have seen the report about his driver being gunned down this morning and a Mafia crew wagon being burned to a hulk."

"Yes, but I never connected it."

"Chief Smith is safe up north a ways in a motel. Looks like it's up to you to run the store for a while."

"They're going to attempt the takeover soon," Jansen said. "When would they have a better chance?"

"With you out of the way. Be careful the next couple of days. Is there any chance you can tie down Captain Davis?"

"I don't know how, other than charging him with a felony of some kind, and for that I'd need proof."

"And he's too slick for that. I'll take care of Captain Davis when I have a few spare minutes. Will you be running things until Chief Smith gets back?"

"I'm the senior, so I guess it's up to me. I'll put out a notice tomorrow that the chief is taking a few days' emergency leave because of his ulcer. He's had one for years and does have to take off a day or two now and then. But what about this takeover try? What are they going to do—blow us all away with bombs or just gun us down?"

"My guess is it'll be more subtle than that. They'll have to get rid of you somehow, so be careful. You might inspect your car before driving home, and be sure you don't get in any car wrecks."

"Or go into any dark warehouses with Captain Davis as my backup," Chief Jansen said.

"Right. Now I've got to get in touch with my contact inside the Mafia machine and see what their next move is going to be."

"You've got a contact inside Nazarione's Mob? How in hell did you do that? I've been trying to do that for five years."

Bolan told him briefly how they turned around the man. By the time the Executioner had finished the story they were back at the spot where Bolan had picked up the chief.

As Jansen got out, Bolan told him he would keep in touch.

"And be careful, Jansen. Don't even trust your best friend."

IT WAS WELL AFTER MIDNIGHT when Don Nazarione met with his number-two man in his third-floor office.

"At least we have some good news," Nazarione said. "Captain Davis tells me the frame-up on Assistant Chief Vincent went off like a military maneuver. The chief is in jail, booked on suspicion of possession of cocaine, theft of cocaine from the police lockup, drinking while driving and a few other charges they're still working on. That eliminates one more. Now there's only Chief Jansen to bother us."

Scimone nodded. "But remember, we need somebody to help run the place who knows how. You don't just wipe out the whole management staff of a new business when you take over. We need one or two down there besides our patsies."

The Mafia boss grunted. "We'll have Davis up as an assistant chief just as soon as possible. There's an opening now."

"Davis said he wants three more men eliminated as soon as possible. We'll worry about that down the line." Scimone took a drag from a long cigar. "What we have to do is give the impression that all is moving along smoothly, that everything is normal and routine. Any changes will have to be done slowly and look reasonable."

The phone rang. At a signal from Carlo, Scimone picked it up. He listened for a minute, then hung up.

"Somebody rammed a pool cue through Jo Jo's heart at that pool palace place. He's in the morgue waiting for an autopsy."

"Bolan?" Nazarione asked.

"Has to be. What about Jo Jo's wife?"

"Send a couple of cars over there and bring her and the two kids over here. She's a handful, and I'd rather a lot of nosy reporters don't get to her. You know how sloshed she usually is."

Scimone moved toward the door.

"I'll go myself. We'll put her and the kids in the south wing. They won't bother you from there."

Nazarione waved and headed for his private elevator. For just a few hours he wanted to get away from business.

Ardly Scimone took one man and a crew wagon and drove to the Albergetti residence. The police had been there, had talked to Angela and left. When Scimone arrived, Angela was lying in the middle of the living room, her blouse open, a drink in her hand, an empty Scotch bottle beside her. They bundled her up with the two kids and took them back to the Nazarione estate.

At first Angela barely said a word. She looked drunk, but in fact the booze had not yet affected her. She stared at Scimone and began swearing. By the time they approached the big house she had worn out her immediate anger.

"I'll kill him!" she shouted. "I'll kill the son of a bitch who did this to my husband. I'll kill him!"

When Angela got out of the car, she couldn't walk. Scimone had to carry her upstairs. The farther he carried her, the more relaxed she became as the alcohol finally took over her body.

Scimone set her on the bed in the wing where she would stay with her children, then hurried out the door. He locked the door from the outside. They were going to have trouble with that one. He had seen widows go this route before. When she sobered up she would be a real hellcat.

9

Mack Bolan had been hunting Captain Davis for over an hour. The captain was still on duty but not in the watch captain's office. He was out investigating some problem or just cruising the town. Bolan had made some purchases earlier in the evening to be ready for a possible showdown. He wanted to handle Davis before he could do any more damage to the Baltimore Police Department.

The Executioner wished he had a police radio so he could contact the captain directly. Instead he phoned.

"Yes, I need to talk to Captain Davis. If you can reach him have him call this number. I'll be here for five minutes. Tell him the name is Bolan." He hung up at once. Now if Davis took the bait, he would come with plenty of backup firepower.

Would he call? Or would he find the location of the phone booth and close in on it? Not enough time for the latter; he would call. Bolan waited by the phone. The booth was in the darkness beside a filling station. He left the door open so no light showed.

Two minutes later the phone rang. Bolan picked it up on the third ring.

"Yes?"

"Bolan! What are you doing in my town?"

"I'm working over the Mafia. I need your help."

"Go on."

"I thought you might give me some inside information on the Mafia operation here."

"Yeah, I could do that. Where can we meet?"

"Just you and me—no other cops involved."

"Sure, sure, no problem."

"You know where Gwynns Falls Park is?"

"Yes."

"Drive there in an unmarked car. Come straight in the main entrance at the far end of the first parking lot. Open your door so the overhead light comes on and wait for me."

"I'd be a perfect target."

"Are you worried? Is someone gunning for you?"

"Of course not, but cops are always targets."

"Your choice. See me there in half an hour or forget it."

"I'll be there."

Bolan ran for his car. He was on the side of town nearest the park, and wanted to be there first. He hoped Davis wouldn't send any patrol cars as backup. He figured not. Davis would know about the head money and would want the five million all to himself.

Ten minutes later, Bolan drove into the green area, eased into the second parking lot and checked out the first. It was too big to set up an easy trap. He filled a two-and-one-half-gallon garden sprayer with the cans of liquid he had bought earlier and set the nozzle to eject a steady stream instead of a spray. Then he sat behind a big maple tree and waited in the moonless night.

Precisely on time, a car rolled through the gate and into the first parking lot. It came to the end and stopped fifty feet north of Bolan. The headlights snapped off and the door opened, spreading light inside the car. It would make Davis almost blind to the outside.

Quietly Bolan moved into the darkness and trailed a three-inch stream of gasoline from one of the cans ten feet behind the unmarked police car. He made a U with the gasoline, pouring it on both sides of the car.

The darkness and the light inside the car let him do the task unseen. He crept into the wooded section at the end of the parking lot, shouldered the heavy sprayer and moved toward the car. He settled behind a wide tree to the right of the car but out of range of the headlights, in case the cop turned them on.

"Davis, is that you?" Bolan called. His voice sounded strangely hollow in the dark outdoors.

A figure stood beside the door.

"Yeah, so let's talk."

"Take out your piece and lay it on top of the car."

"Hey, you don't ask a cop to give up his weapon."

"I do. I'm allergic to cops. But you're safe with me, you know that."

There was a pause, then a sound of metal against metal. Bolan figured Davis would also have a hidden weapon.

"You've been lucky so far, Davis. You've got away with everything. First the two thousand a month bribe money you're taking from Don Nazarione, then the snuff on Lieutenant Paulson, and the blackmail on the two assistant chiefs. You even pulled off the cocaine plant on Chief Vincent."

"What the hell are you talking about?"

"You, Davis. You're just dirty as hell. Do you want to give up all this and turn state's evidence against Nazarione and his killers? If you do, we can save you from the death penalty."

"You're insane. I'm a cop. Six awards for valor, three commendations. I didn't come out here to be insulted."

"Don't leave just yet." Bolan drew Big Thunder and put one heavy .44 round from the AutoMag into the police car's engine, then another. "Your wheels just died on you, Davis." He struck a match, lit the remaining nineteen matches in the book and threw the flaming cardboard torch into the dark stain of gasoline on the tarmac.

There came an immediate whooshing sound as the gasoline and the vapor burst into flame. The trail of fire raced around the U shape he had poured.

Davis screamed and fired two shots from a handgun. Bolan, wedged behind a tree, pumped up the sprayer, triggered the nozzle and sent a stream of gasoline into the closest trail of flames. Quickly he laid down a gasoline line in front of the car, closing the box of flames around the car.

Davis fired again, missed and yelled.

"What the hell you doing? I came out here to help you!"

"You came out here to kill me and collect the reward from the Mafia commission. It isn't going to work."

Bolan sent a dozen shots of the gasoline at Davis, who stood beside the car. In a few seconds his clothes were soaked with gasoline.

"Now, Davis, you try to run through that ring of fire and you go up in flames. Let's get practical. You answer some questions and I might not kill you."

"Go to hell, Bolan! I'll get inside the car."

"Then I'll shoot at the gas tank and set the car on fire."

Davis had started to get in the car. Now he stopped. Through the snapping of the flames, Bolan heard Davis sigh.

"Okay. What questions do you have?"

"When is the takeover try on the police department?"

Davis inhaled sharply. "How did you know about that?"

"Doesn't matter now. When is it?"

"They haven't told me for sure yet. It's soon."

"How many cops does Nazarione have on the take?"

"How many... probably three hundred or so. He doesn't tell me that."

"Why was Chief Smith killed?"

"Because he was not the kind who could be turned around to our way of thinking."

Bolan used the sprayer again to increase the fire surrounding the car, then sprayed Davis again before he slid inside the car.

"Just a reminder, Davis. You're not fireproof."

"Fuck you, Bolan." The cop fired two shots; both missed. The Executioner moved behind the tree. He knew he had to get around behind the rig and spray a new line yet stay out of the light.

He walked deeper into the brush, then ran to one side and sprayed the fire line again. The gasoline burst into flames in the air and worked back toward the nozzle, but Bolan stopped the stream.

Two more shots came, one nicking the metal sprayer tank.

The fire line vanished for six feet across the back of the U.

Bolan ran toward it. He sensed the cop making a dash for it, too. There was not enough time for the Executioner to run there and reestablish the flames.

Instead he turned and drew a new line closer to the car, directly in front of the running cop. The thin line of fire and the lawman got to the same point simultaneously. After a second, Davis's saturated clothing burst into flames.

Davis screamed.

Bolan stopped squirting and stared.

Davis became a six-foot torch. The flames shot up his pant legs and across his jacket in one whooshing vapor explosion. His hair sparked like fireworks in tiny balls of flames, then burst into fire as he screamed and tried to beat it out with his hands.

Somehow he had lived through the vapor explosion when the oxygen in the air around him had been sucked into the fire. Now he staggered and fell, trying to roll. His screams came one on top of another.

As he rolled, the fire snuffed out under him, but as soon as the air hit his clothing again the gasoline reignited and burned fiercely, as only a petroleum fire can.

Davis rolled again and again. His hand came out, seeking help.

For a moment in the firelight, Bolan saw the captain's face clearly. His eyebrows were gone, his hair was blackened stubble, his ears were on fire. Now his eyes made one last frantic appeal. Then his hand fell, and his lungs filled with the inhaled gasoline vapor. Flames danced over his body. The vapor in his lungs exploded and Capt. Harley Davis's chest erupted outward, blowing vital organs onto the pavement and snuffing out any life that had persisted through the twenty seconds of the immolation.

Bolan returned to the woods beyond the parking lot. Already the fire was going out. Scraps of clothing on the body only smoldered once the gasoline had burned away.

The Executioner dropped the sprayer and moved through the woods toward the second parking lot. Hearing sirens, he ran, started his Buick and drove out the far park entrance and continued slowly back toward town.

Davis had had a choice. He could have cooperated if he had wanted to. Essentially he'd killed himself. Bolan had only made it convenient for him to do so.

Somewhere along the drive, Bolan peeled from his hands the thin surgeon's gloves he had worn during the confrontration and threw them out the window.

He still did not know when the takeover would be attempted, but realized it would be gradual. The public would not stand for a coup. The Mafia had its fangs so deeply into the department now that the takeover was almost complete. But Bolan figured they were planning a day or an event to wrap it up. He would find that out tomorrow.

He drove back to his small hotel and slept until dawn.

10

Mack Bolan crouched behind a tree next to the Nazarione estate. He had been up with the morning sun, checked with Nino Tattaglia and found out that the Mafia turncoat still did not know when the final thrust of the Mafia's takeover of the police department would occur.

Bolan had to know today. So he planned a lightning raid on the godfather's own fortress by daylight. He knew just enough about the layout to get by. If he was lucky, and no one tried to be a hero, he would succeed.

Then there was his ace in the hole. He watched a guard patrol the cement fence. The sentry made the circuit every twelve minutes. Such punctuality could get him killed. Bolan waited until he had passed, then looked into the parking area behind the mansion, where four crew wagons sat.

Nothing big was scheduled for this morning, or the wagons would be in front ready for loading. A mechanic came out, tinkered with one of the engines for a minute, then slammed the hood and went into the big house.

The Executioner looked at the cars, hoping that at least one of those in which he had planted the radio-detonated bombs was in the group below. There was only one way to find out.

It was time. Bolan took out the small black box, opened it and thumbed a toggle switch to the On position. There was no one around the crew wagons. He put his finger on the red button and pushed.

Immediately the peaceful neighborhood was rocked by a pair of explosions from the parking area. One of the crew wagons lifted off the ground and came down with its rear wheels on top of another Cadillac. The second blast tore another crew wagon in half, throwing the engine and front section ten feet across the yard, leaving the rest of the body and rear wheels where they had been.

While the debris was still falling, men ran out of the house and garage. People were everywhere. The guards charged into the area, their handguns out and ready.

As Bolan hoped, the sentries had left their posts, and he scaled the wall and hid behind the shrubbery that would give him cover and a safe route all the way to the mansion.

He made the run without attracting attention. Then he heard someone shouting at the guards to return to their posts.

Bolan rose and examined the closest window. It was locked from the inside. Breaking it would make too much noise. As he stared, a woman appeared, looked back at him, grinned and raised the window.

"Looking for a way inside?" she asked.

It took Bolan that long to recognize Angela Albergetti, Jo Jo's widow. Now she wore a blouse, and her blond hair was combed, brushed and set beautifully.

"Come on in before they find you. We wouldn't want to get blood all over that nice sport shirt."

Bolan went over the sill and into the room. He was on his feet at once, and she stood in front of him.

"That should be worth at least a thank-you. I know I've seen you somewhere before, but I can't quite place you. Oh, I'm Angela."

He nodded.

She laughed. "Well, are you going to say hello, or blow up the rest of the house? You made a good start on the motor pool out there."

"Hello, Angela. The house is safe. That was what we call a strategic diversion."

"I don't know who you are, but I like you. And I'm not overly delighted with the management right now. They moved me out of my house because they thought I'd shout everything I knew about these guys to reporters. I just might have. They got my old man killed yesterday or the day before. Sometime." She looked up and shrugged. "Whatever. What's your line of work?"

"I help people to change their minds about things."

"I'm ready."

"Later. First I need to do some research upstairs."

"In Don Carlo's office?"

"Right. And I'll have to come back through here when I'm done."

She nodded.

Bolan smiled and moved silently, swiftly to the hall door. This was the south wing. He had to get to the main wing, third floor. He hesitated at the door.

"Want me to show you the way?"

"Yes, and be a cover for me."

"Hey, this could be fun. I want to see Carlo's surprise when you walk in."

"He should be in the motor pool by then. Let's go."

They moved down the hall, upstairs to the third floor and to a connecting door that led into the main wing. No one was on duty outside the godfather's sanctum.

Bolan knocked, waited, then opened the door and slid inside, leaving Angela in the hall.

The room looked as it had before. Now there was an unfinished handwritten letter on the desk, and behind it a big chart on a bulletin board.

Bolan stared at it, then studied the names on lines under it. Three assistant chiefs of police were listed, along with Chief Smith and Lieutenant Paulson. At the bottom of the chart were a number of dates, but one had been circled. Tomorrow! On a note beside it was a phrase. "At the Mayor's State of the City Speech."

Bolan checked some file drawers and the desk, but found nothing that would be helpful. He decided it was time to haul ass, as he used to say in the army.

He eased open the office door and peered out. A Mafia soldier with his back to the door was talking to Angela.

The Executioner swung open the door, surged out and brought the side of the Beretta down across the soldier's skull. The man turned and collapsed, out cold. Bolan caught him and eased him to the floor.

"Let's get out of here!" Bolan whispered.

They ran lightly down the hall, through the access door and into the other hallway. Then they walked past a maid, whose arms were full of rumpled sheets, and a minute later were safely in Angela's room.

"They'll find that goon quickly and you'll be in trouble," the Executioner said.

She smiled. "Then you'll just have to take me with you or they'll do all sorts of ugly things to me."

Bolan scowled for a moment, then shrugged. "Do you have any pants? It's easier going out windows and over walls in pants than in a skirt."

"I'll have to change."

"I've seen ladies change clothes before."

"Yes, I'll just bet you have." She took a suitcase from a stand and pawed through it, found a pair of tan pants and a tan blouse. She watched him closely as she removed her blouse. When he remained silent, she dropped her skirt, revealing skimpy blue panties. A moment later she shrugged and put on the blouse, then the pants and slipped into a pair of worn running shoes.

"If you want to wait until it gets dark, we could think of something to do to pass the time."

"Sounds interesting, but I have a deadline. Raise the window and look around. Are they still looking at the cars?"

She raised the window. There was no screen.

"I see only a pair of guards."

"Figures."

Bolan stood well back in the room and looked outside. It was going to be harder to leave than it had been to arrive. He had no more diversions. The bombs planted in the house would have to wait for another time. Getting the woman out would make it tougher—unless he used her as a diversion.

Briefly he outlined an idea to her and she giggled.

"I love it! I haven't had so much fun since I went skinny-dipping in the pool of the Beverly Hills Hotel."

Watching at the window they timed the rounds of the guards. When the way was clear, they slid out through the opening. Bolan pulled the window shut and led Angela through the shrubs down to the tennis-court trail, where there was a gap in the brush.

They waited in the shrubs until a young guard approached, carrying an Uzi. The timing was critical. As the guard came near, Angela stepped out of the brush.

She jumped with feigned surprise and turned around. In the few seconds it took him to recover, Bolan rose out of the brush and brought the hardened edge of his palm down on the man's neck. The man dropped and the Executioner dragged him into the shrubbery. Then he and Angela crossed to the far side of the walk, hidden again.

At the path near the fence, Angela sat on a patch of grass in the sunshine and opened her blouse for a little bit of all-over tan. The first guard to approach cleared his throat about twenty feet away. She pretended to be sleeping as she leaned against the wall. The guard walked quietly by, staring. He did not see Bolan rising behind him.

The Executioner swung the Uzi submachine gun he had confiscated from the other guard, smashing it against the side of the man's neck. His neck cracked loudly. When the criminal soldier collapsed, he would never rise again.

Bolan boosted the woman over the six-foot block wall, then went over himself. They slumped against the wall, then as a neighbor's dog barked, they calmly walked to the street and Bolan's rented Buick.

Three miles away, Bolan pulled to a curb.

"What now?" Angela asked.

"That's up to you. You've escaped. Can I drive you somewhere?"

"No, I like it here with you."

"I have some work to finish. Do you have any relatives where I can take you?"

"No, just back to Carlo's castle."

Bolan turned around, opened the suitcase on the rear seat and slid the Uzi inside. Before he could stop her, Angela grabbed a grenade. She held the arming handle down and pulled the ring, removing the safety pin.

She sat in the passenger side of the car, holding the grenade in her right hand, a strange, wild look on her pretty face.

"I finally remembered where I saw you before. It was at our house the night Jo Jo died. Hell, he wasn't much, but he was mine! He fathered my children. What am I supposed to do now—live off the goodness of the godfather for the next sixty years?"

She did not wait for a reply. "No way! I'll work the streets first, selling my ass! Then here you come, the

WOULD YOU BELIEVE THESE MEN CAN HOLD YOU CAPTIVE IN YOUR OWN HOME?

MAIL THIS STICKER TODAY

WE'LL SEND YOU
4 FREE BOOKS
JUST TO PROVE IT.
See inside for details.

Discover Gold Eagle's power to keep you spellbound . . .

WITHOUT CHARGE OR OBLIGATION

Good books are hard to find. And hard men are good to find. We've got both.

Gold Eagle books are so good, so hard, so exciting that we guarantee they'll keep you riveted to your chair until their fiery conclusion.

That's because you don't just read a Gold Eagle novel . . . you *live* it.

Your blood will race as you join *Mack Bolan* and his high-powered combat squads—*Able Team*, *Phoenix Force*, *Track* and *SOBs*—in their relentless crusade against worldwide terror. You'll feel the pressure build page after page until the nonstop action explodes in a high-voltage climax of vengeance and retribution against mankind's most treacherous criminals.

Get 4 electrifying novels— FREE

To prove Gold Eagle delivers the most pulse-pounding, pressure-packed action reading ever published, we'll send you

4 novels— **ABSOLUTELY FREE.**

If you like them, we'll send you 6 brand-new books every other month to preview. Always before they're available in stores. Always at a hefty saving off the retail price. Always with the right to cancel and owe nothing.

As a Gold Eagle subscriber, you'll also receive . . .
- our free newsletter, AUTOMAG, with each shipment
- special books to preview free and buy at a deep discount

Get a digital watch— FREE

Return the attached Card today, and we'll also send you a digital quartz calendar watch FREE. It comes complete with a long-life battery and a one-year warranty (excluding battery). *Like the 4 free books, it's yours to keep even if you never buy another Gold Eagle book.*

RUSH YOUR ORDER TO US TODAY

YOU CAN'T PUT
A GOOD BOOK DOWN

Razor-edged stories ripped from today's headlines. Page-crackling tension. Spine-chilling adventure. Adrenaline-pumping excitement. Do-or-die heroes. Gold Eagle books slam home raw action the way you want it—hard, fast and real.

big killer, the man who made me a widow. At least I remember, and I know I have to do something about it. Guns are hard to use. You can miss when you try to kill someone. But a grenade! There's no chance to miss. So what if I have to stay here with you to make sure? I just let the handle pop off and I hold it right in your gut and blow both of us all over the inside of this car!'' Her eyes were wild and she was breathing fast. She reached down and rubbed her breast.

"I'll blow us both to hell! Better that way. Damn sight better that way. Carlo can raise my two kids.''

Bolan knew she was very near to doing what she threatened to do. He had seen angry women before. He moved toward her slowly, and rested his hand on her shoulder. He patted her gently as she rambled on.

"Hell, I don't care. I got cheated out of a husband. Somebody who treated me fine in spite of the bitchy things I did to him. That man was a saint.''

Bolan moved closer, speaking softly. He knew she was distraught and any sudden moves on his part could mean the end for both of them.

"Angela, I know things look a little gloomy now,'' Bolan coaxed, "but they'll be better. Think of your children!''

He caught her hand gently and eased the grenade away while holding the arming handle firmly in place.

Bolan leaned away from her, took a roll of black tape from the suitcase on the seat behind them and taped the grenade's arming handle solidly in position. Then he put it back in the case.

She sighed and broke into tears. "Oh, damn! I have to go back. I'll tell Carlo that you tricked me and forced me to help you, and that I almost killed you with a grenade. He'll have to believe me."

Bolan reached over, touched her chin and turned her face to him.

"Angela, you are a beautiful, sexy woman. Just relax and see how things look in a month or so. You'll be married again within a year, or I miss my guess."

She blinked. "You really think so?"

"Yes, besides, killing me won't accomplish anything. Your children must be important to you."

"Yes, of course. But I'm important, too."

He dropped her downtown and watched her get a cab. The women were the real losers within the whole Mafia framework, he thought. The mobsters' women always lost.

He consulted his watch—not quite noon. There was a little more than twenty-four hours before the mayor's speech. He had a lot of important work to do before then.

Behind the rented Buick, a man in a rented Thunderbird watched Mack Bolan. The man was large—six foot four and 260 pounds of hardened muscle. He had black flashing eyes, dark hair that crowded his collar and was clean shaven. His name was Vince Carboni and he worked for *La Commissione*, the high commission of the Mafia bosses of bosses. His only job— to hunt down and kill Mack Bolan.

11

Vince Carboni snorted as he watched the man he had been hunting for two months. Now he would watch Mack Bolan, get in position and blow him away before Bolan even knew that Vince Carboni was in town.

He had been going to see Carlo Nazarione to warn him not to notify the Bolan Search Center in New York that the bastard was in Baltimore. Turning in at Nazarione's gate, he saw two people walking down the street. One was a knockout blonde, the other one was Bolan.

Carboni had slowly passed to make certain, then circled the block and followed the pair to a car. They drove around and then stopped and talked. Later they drove downtown, where the woman got out and hailed a taxi.

Pure chance that he had spotted Mack Bolan, but he'd take it.

When Bolan's Buick pulled away from the curb, Carboni's Thunderbird followed two cars behind. He had practiced following cars around New York; if you can tail a car in Manhattan, you can stay with one anywhere. Carboni was an expert. As long as the victim did not know he was being followed, Carboni usually stayed three or four cars behind. If the other guy knew, it became a race, not a tail.

Carboni knew at once that Bolan had no idea he was being tailed. The Buick sedan wound through several streets, then stopped near a phone booth. Carboni parked across the one-way street and watched.

He had been waiting a long time for this chance. The commission first came to him a year ago. He had been happy working in New York as an enforcer and "eliminator," as they called it now. But the commission offered him ten times the money he was making, and his own don urged him to take the job, so there was no problem either way.

He spent two months on weapons, learning everything he could about handguns, all the auto and semiauto submachine guns, and then taking a postgraduate course from an old sapper about gunk, juice, powder and plastic explosives.

For two weeks he spent sixteen hours a day reading everything the commission had collected on the Executioner. They had copies of every story printed in the United States.

Slowly Carboni filtered out fiction from fact, the hype and local paranoia from the reality. He knew more about Mack Bolan, his family, his involvement with the government at Stony Man Farm and his subsequent "disengagement" from Uncle Sam than anyone in the Mafia.

Now he planned to kill Bolan!

Carboni had missed the bastard in Portland, but just barely. This time he would not miss. It was a matter of pride now.

There was only one restraint. Vince Carboni was not going to sacrifice his own life just to get the Executioner. He could not spend that five-million reward if he were laid out in a coffin. Which was why he did not unlimber his .44 AutoMag right then and blast Bolan as he stood in the phone booth. Not with a hundred witnesses to identify both him and the car. He was too smart for that.

Bolan left the phone booth and drove north. He hit the Jones Falls Expressway and continued north across the Beltway. The small town of Brooklandville was ahead. It was almost rural here, a few small farms and acreages. Traffic fell to nothing. Carboni pulled up behind the Buick and leaned out the window. There was no chance now to disguise a tail, but at least there would be damn few witnesses out here.

His first shot blew the left rear tire. The Buick moved sideways, then back, as it stopped on the right shoulder.

Carboni braked the T-Bird to a halt fifty yards behind and ducked. He went out the side door and saw that the Buick's door was open, too.

Beyond a small ditch was a field of corn, head high. Bolan was out there somewhere.

Carboni jumped back in the car as a small-caliber shot thunked into the door where he had crouched. He went out the door on the other side and stared into the cornfield. Before he could determine a strategy, the boom of an AutoMag broke the silence and the rented

Thunderbird rocked as the heavy round crashed into the engine. He heard steam escaping and swore.

His wheels were probably dead! Carboni charged around the back of the car, raced across the ditch and into the cornfield. He paused in the corn, breathing heavily, then held his breath and listened.

All he heard was leaves rustling in the breeze. Where the hell was Bolan? He looked down the row, but the lush growth of the stalks and leaves obscured the view beyond about a dozen feet in any direction. He looked over the top of the six-foot tassels, but saw no one.

Carboni moved deeper into the field toward the spot where he supposed Bolan had to be. All he wanted was one good shot. Just one and he would collect five million dollars!

The hit man eased forward again, then stopped. He heard an engine grind, catch and wheels spin. Carboni screamed and reversed, running wildly through the corn, holding the AutoMag ready.

The damn Executioner had slipped back to the Buick and was moving.

Carboni saw the Buick drive along the shoulder, its back tire flopping. His .44 AutoMag ejected three rounds into the side windows. Then a round hit the gas tank. Gas gushed out but did not explode.

Carboni was running as fast as the car was flopping along. He charged along the ditch, figuring the rig could not move more than three or four hundred yards with only the fuel in the carburetor and fuel pump.

After a hundred yards the Buick wavered, and the engine sputtered and died. Carboni went flat on the ground in the ditch and waited for Bolan to step out and die.

A minute later, the hit man frowned. Bolan had not yet emerged from the car.

Fifty yards behind Carboni, Mack Bolan knelt among the cornstalks, clipping grenades onto his hastily donned combat harness and web belt. He adjusted his AutoMag and put the Uzi on its shoulder strap. Then he moved toward the road, the Uzi up and waiting.

Carboni had crawled along the ditch to the Buick. He walked around the Buick, his big gun ready.

Bolan grinned, wishing he could see the expression on the big headhunter's face. His contacts told him that Vince Carboni, a former hit man from New York, was smart, mean and resourceful, and had spent three months training before starting the manhunt for Mack Bolan.

Vince Carboni was not a man to take lightly.

He would be furious when he found the Buick's steering wheel tied down and a big rock on the gas pedal.

When the New York gunner came behind the Buick, Bolan slammed a 5-round burst at him from the Uzi. The mafioso ducked, and the rounds pounded into the Buick.

Bolan's combat-trained mind had evaluated his options and selected one computer-fast—search and destroy. He needed to eliminate this continuing threat.

Bolan darted up to Carboni's Thunderbird and looked inside. A Weatherby Mark V rifle lay on the back seat. The Executioner removed the weapon and retreated to the rear of the car. Sheltered behind the car, he decided he could not carry the ten-and-one-half-pound weapon. He quickly took the bolt from the big rifle, making it inoperative, threw the rifle into the cornfield and the bolt in the opposite direction.

Then he moved forward. The Mafia hit man was next on the Executioner's own hit list.

As Bolan ran for the cornfield, three rounds snapped past him. There were from Carboni's AutoMag, and now he knew how others felt when he fired his own big gun at them and missed. He charged into the corn, moved inward fifty feet, then carefully worked forward. He tried but could not entirely prevent the tops and tassels of the cornstalks from swaying as he moved from one row to another.

Something black flew through the air toward him.

Grenade! He charged twenty feet down the row, then dived into the soft dirt as the bomb exploded. The inch-thick cornstalks absorbed most of the shrapnel. He had seen the bomb just in time.

One fragger was left in the suitcase in the Buick. What else? Only a .45 and some extra ammo for his weapons. So the fragger probably had been one of his own. He would find out shortly. He moved cautiously toward the road without disturbing a single leaf.

Bolan stopped at the edge of the corn, still concealed. He checked each way and at last saw Carboni behind the dead Thunderbird; one of his legs showed under the car. A 6-round burst from Bolan's Uzi brought a scream from the mob goon. The hit man fired over the car into the cornfield with no idea where his target was.

Bolan was running short of ammo for the Uzi, which he had taken from the guard at Carlo's castle. He had two more magazines and that was it. He had to conserve his firepower, since the Uzi was the only long gun in the contest.

Carboni crossed the road, then limped to a fence and crawled under it. By the time Bolan saw him he was a quarter mile away, crossing a pasture toward a dry irrigation ditch.

Sprinting, the Executioner moved the Uzi to single shot and sent two rounds into the ditch where Carboni had vanished. He scanned the area. The irrigation ditch ran toward some farm buildings a mile away, set in the middle of what might once have been a mile-square farm. A small stream with lots of brush and small trees growing along it meandered through the pasture and came within two hundred yards of the barn.

Why was Carboni heading for the buildings? Again Bolan's combat-trained mind checked off the possibilities and came up with the most reasonable. The thug was hurt and looking for shelter, a longer weapon and possibly hostages to use for bargaining.

Bolan did not like any of these motives. He ran toward the barn, hoping to intercept the hit man before he reached it.

The shot came without warning. It lanced through the air less than three feet from Bolan, and he dived and rolled into a slight depression in the pasture. The second shot missed his head by a foot. Carboni had traveled faster than Bolan had anticipated, and was firing from fifty feet ahead of him.

So much for the first tactic. On his toes and elbows, keeping his body just off the ground, Bolan crawled toward the creek and its cover of brush and trees.

He made it to the creek, taking only one more shot from Carboni, who had worked farther down the irrigation ditch. Carboni would beat him to the barn and the other buildings. That could be a real problem.

Bolan waded across the foot-deep creek and began running along the meandering stream toward the barn, still three hundred yards ahead of him.

He was still fifty yards from where the creek came closest to the barn, when he saw Carboni jump out of the ditch and race for the protection of the wooden structure.

Bolan hoped there was no one home. Maybe they were all out in the fields. As if denying his hope, a screen door slammed somewhere.

Bolan worked out a new tactical plan. He would swing around the barn to the house. He ran hard.

Panting after the four hundred yards, he approached the sixteen or twenty fruit trees behind the house, most large enough to give him some protection.

He took no enemy fire.

Again he dashed from one tree to the next, edging closer to the old two-story frame farmhouse. There was no back door. He knelt behind a bushy apple tree closest to the house. From there he walked casually, the Uzi at his side. He hoped no one would glance out the rear windows.

As he reached the house he heard the roar of an AutoMag. A scream followed. He hit the ground, edged to the corner of the house and looked around.

Thirty feet away, Carboni held a woman around the waist and pulled her close to him. In his right hand was the big cannon. The two figures walked forward and out of sight around the front of the house.

Bolan sprinted to the next corner, and saw a man sprawled on the grass by a wooden gate. Bolan knew he was dead. The mobster must be inside the house with the woman. Kids? Probably. The woman looked to be in her thirties.

The Executioner peered in a window on the side of the house. In a large kitchen with a long wooden table, Carboni sat on a bench, his gun pointed at the woman, who was bandaging Carboni's calf with some cloth. Behind them a baby sat in a high chair, and two children about six and eight sat rigidly on the far side of the table.

Carboni said something to the woman, who went to a refrigerator and brought out cold cuts. The man was not going to move for a while, but maybe he could be faked outside.

Bolan drew the Beretta 93-R and worked around the front of the house, moving below windows until he was four feet from the open screen door. He cupped his hands around his mouth.

"Carboni!" Bolan called. "This place is surrounded by our SWAT team. Come out with your hands up and you won't be shot."

The Executioner heard movement inside the house, then a woman's light steps running up some stairs. Heavier footsteps came toward the door.

"Damn! Nobody out there. Must have been that bastard Bolan!"

The steps retreated, and the Executioner went to the kitchen window and looked in. The three kids sat where they had been. The woman was gone.

Carboni grabbed the six-year-old and held him against his chest. The big .44 AutoMag muzzle pressed on the boy's head.

"Farm lady. You come down here in ten seconds or I'm gonna blow this kid of yours right straight to hell!"

"No!" she screamed and came running into the room, a deer rifle still in her hands. She dropped the weapon and held out her arms.

Carboni kept the child. "Sit down and shut up. There's a guy outside gunning for me, and I'm aiming to make him dead before I leave this place. You got a shotgun?"

The woman shook her head.

"Quit lying, bitch! You like this kid or don't you?"

"Yes, I forgot! It's in the cupboard, right over there."

"Bring it and a box of shells over here. Do it now, lady. I ain't got nothing against you but I don't like you, either. Means not a damn thing to me whether the rest of your family lives or dies. Understand?"

"Yes." The woman put the double-barreled shotgun and a box of shells on the table beside him.

"And finish that goddamn sandwich. You put anything in there that you wouldn't eat yourself, and I blow this kid's brains all over you and the kitchen."

Even through the window, Bolan could see the strain on the woman. She was short and brunette, and now her face was frozen tight with terror. She made a sandwich of cheese and ham and lettuce, and another one of tuna and put them in front of Carboni with a can of beer.

"Two more beers," he said. He ate with his left hand, his right holding the weapon against the boy.

Bolan had no chance for a kill shot. Even a head shot would give the hoodlum time to pull the trigger, killing the boy. There was no device on his combat harness that would help him rout the man out of the kitchen.

He checked the grenades and remembered he had brought one flash-stun grenade for a test. He had never used it. He balanced out the possible damage the concussion might do the baby. The stun effect would be far less harmful than a round from Carboni's big .44.

Carboni would not leave witnesses. He would kill without a thought if he figured it would help him even slightly. After all, hadn't he already murdered the man of the family?

The Executioner moved to the front door and looked inside. Could he get down the hall to the kitchen without being heard? He made sure his equipment wouldn't rattle, then pulled the pin on the flash-stun grenade and dropped it on the grass. He held the arming spoon around the grenade tightly and eased onto the first step.

Gingerly he pushed the handle on the aluminum screen door. It moved without a sound. He pulled it open a foot, slipped through and let it touch his back and close gently as he started down the hall. He had the Beretta up and on single shot. There were too many innocents in there to be spraying bullets.

Step by step, he worked down the hall, which had been resurfaced with ceramic tile—no squeaks. He pressed against the left wall, since this was the side the killer could not see.

He was halfway down when the woman, walking to the refrigerator, turned and stared straight at him. Either she was too surprised to react or had great control. She lifted her brows slightly and walked out of sight.

She must have instantly realized he was on her side. There had been no time to whisper anything or mouth any words.

He moved forward. Now he could hear the sounds from the room. The baby whimpered.

"He's wet. Can I take him out and change him?"

"No, he won't melt. Just shut him up."

A beer can hit the table.

There was a chance the man would release the boy and go after Bolan, but the Executioner doubted it. This guy was a professional. He would take every advantage he could.

At the edge of the doorway, Bolan could see half of the kitchen, but the table and the people were in the other half. He would throw the flash-stun grenade near the table. Pitch it and hope. If the hit man got Bolan, the rest of the family was dead, anyway. He had to take the chance.

The Executioner wanted to look inside, but knew he couldn't risk it. He was ready. Kneeling, he brought up the Beretta and let the arming handle pop loose in his hand. Two seconds later, he lobbed the grenade into the room.

It exploded almost as it hit the floor.

Bolan had closed his eyes and put his hands over his ears, and saw the flash through his eyelids. Then he charged into the room.

The blast was louder than anything Bolan had heard outside a war zone for a long time. The baby screamed. Carboni dropped his AutoMag, then grabbed the woman. Both blinded, they stumbled backward, but Carboni remained covered by the woman. Bolan had no sure shot.

"Bastard!" Carboni screamed. He produced a knife from his pocket and opened it into a five-inch murderously sharp blade.

"Move a step, Bolan, and I gut her. You want that? Move and she and the kids are dead. You got that, bastard?"

He was still blind, stalling for time. Bolan aimed at the only sure target, his right shoulder, and the knife fell from his hand. Carboni screamed and hunched behind the woman, one hand around her throat. He stumbled toward the door into the living room.

"Stay there, Bolan, or I'll rip out her carotid artery."

Bolan lifted the baby, gave him to the girl and hurried the children out of the house. They ran toward the barn.

Bolan returned inside just in time to grab the shotgun and realize the .44 was no longer on the floor where it had fallen. The Executioner heard something and dived just as the big .44 AutoMag like his own fired twice in rapid succession.

12

The first bullet missed Bolan by inches. The second slammed into his left arm and then out. An inch lower and it would have broken the bone. He was lucky to get only a surface wound.

His Beretta stuttered out three rounds in return, chipping away at the doorframe through which the commission's hit man had vanished. Bolan bolted through the kitchen into the living room. The hit man and his hostage had moved to the back hall, near a bedroom.

The woman screamed.

"You just lost your advantage, Carboni."

"I've got the woman."

"You kill her, what do you have left?"

"You won't let her die."

"Don't count on it," said Bolan. "Go ahead and blow her away. That will make my job of killing you that much easier."

The only answer was silence. Bolan heard a muffled scream, then a window shatter. The Executioner sprinted out the front door and around to the back. Carboni, dragging the woman, was running for the barn. Bolan fired into the air, the woman fell and clawed at Carboni until he released her.

The Mafia's hireling turned and sighted the heavy pistol at Bolan. Knowing how accurate the AutoMag was, Bolan dived to one side and rolled. He came up with the Uzi ready and sprayed a dozen rounds, then zigzagged for the barn. Another three shots from Carboni missed him. Carboni dived through the barn doorway. The woman ran back to the house.

Bolan retreated to a cement well house, six feet square, that stood between the barn and the house. The woman left the house and ran to the well.

She was frantic, her eyes wild, her hands clawing the air.

"Where are my babies?" she screamed at the Executioner.

"They left the house," Bolan said. "I think they went to the barn."

"But that monster is there!"

The hayloft door swung out and clattered against the side of the barn. From the shadows inside came Carboni's voice.

"I have three hostages now, Bolan. Here's what you're going to do. You're going to throw out your weapons one by one, and then stand in the middle of the yard. If you don't do that in twenty seconds, I'm going to take this little girl and smash her skull against this post, then toss her out."

"No! No! No!" the woman screamed. Bolan grabbed her and pulled her behind the well.

"Listen to me!" he said to her, staring into her face. "He'll do exactly that if I stay here. So I'm going to run into the fields. If he wants me, he'll have to leave the kids here. When he goes, get the kids away. If you don't have a car, run for it in the opposite direction. Don't stay here. Understand?''

The woman nodded. Tears streamed down her face.

''Just don't let him hurt my babies!'' she whispered.

Bolan took out his .44 AutoMag and put two shots through the hayloft door.

''Give me a minute, then yell to him that I ran into the fields through the apple orchard. He'll leave. Stay hidden until he's gone.'' She was shivering. He hugged her tightly. ''Your kids will be fine. Just do what I told you.''

Bolan put one more round through the hayloft opening, then turned and ran. Just past the house, Carboni fired the big .44 at him but missed. Bolan jogged behind the house and continued. He had to get the maniac away from the children.

He ran to the stream and splashed across, continuing into the brush on the far side, occasionally splashing back across the little creek. He still had his three weapons but was not sure how he could use them out here.

Hearing an unusual noise, he turned and saw a tractor bouncing across the field. It came to a fence and plowed through it, knocking down posts and snapping barbed wire.

Bolan stopped running but stayed hidden in the brush.

Two minutes later he saw that the tractor was being driven by Carboni. Rolling along at ten or twelve miles an hour, it was soon entering Bolan's range of fire.

"Just a little closer," Bolan said, urging the killer to swing toward the creek. The Uzi was good for accurate firing at more than 200 yards, but the closer the better, and the target was still 150 yards away. He steadied the Uzi on a small log and sent five rounds toward the bouncing tractor. They slammed into the tractor but missed the driver.

Carboni was moving off the seat as the second spray of 9 mm parabellums slashed toward him. One must have hit him because he fell off the tractor. When it chugged by, he was nowhere to be seen. The tractor kept on going until the engine coughed and died fifty yards down the field.

Bolan fired into the tall grass just to the left of the spot he had last seen Carboni, then rolled to his right on instinct. A .44 round sang through the trees.

That gave the Executioner an idea. He picked a sturdy small tree and climbed fifteen feet high.

Now he could see the flattened grass where Carboni had slithered away. Evidently he had crawled toward a farm road half a mile away. A small depression opened into a little ravine, and Bolan saw that it soon became deep enough to hide Carboni as he ran.

The Executioner climbed down and ran along the high ground, certain he could find a spot somewhere ahead where he could pin down the Mafia hoodlum in the low ground.

There came a scream as of an animal in mortal danger. Bolan ran over a small rise and peered into the gully. Three hundred yards ahead Carboni was lying in the grass, struggling with something on his foot.

The Executioner fired twice toward the hoodlum, not expecting a hit.

Carboni screamed again, tore something off his foot and limped into the brush along the stream in the narrow valley.

A hundred yards farther, he climbed the bank, then disappeared over a ridge, evidently working toward the country road.

Bolan ran, cutting through the ravine to see what had given Carboni trouble.

It was a steel-jawed animal trap, now with blood on its teeth. It could easily have broken Carboni's ankle. At least it would slow him down.

The Executioner ran up the hill, made certain Carboni was not waiting to ambush him at the top, then went over the ridge along a different route than the Mafia killer had taken.

Limping, Carboni was well down the slope, angling for the road. Down the road about a mile, Bolan could see a pickup truck approaching. Carboni saw it, too, and hurried to get to the road before it passed.

Bolan wished he had brought the Weatherby Mark V instead of the Uzi. With the Mark V he could have picked Carboni off at half a mile.

Bolan ran forward, surprised at the strength and determination of the wounded man in front of him, yet hardly aware of his own injured arm. Carboni ran hard the last hundred yards and stumbled onto the macadam roadway before the pickup arrived. He dropped to his knees and waved.

Billy Olsen saw the man running toward the road and slowed. As the man fell to his knees and waved, the year-old pickup slammed to a stop.

Billy's wife, Faye, frowned.

"We're gonna be late, Billy."

"Man needs help. Got blood on his leg."

He turned off the engine, stepped out of the rig and went around the front.

"Looks like you could use some help, mister," he said.

"Sure as hell can," Carboni said, swinging the big AutoMag around and killing Billy Olsen with one shot through the heart.

Faye screamed and moved to start the pickup. But the keys were in her dead husband's pocket.

Carboni saw her and laughed.

"Need keys, lady. Don't worry, I'm not going to hurt you. I just want your rig. Get out."

He took the keys from the dead man's right-hand pocket and returned to the pickup. He knew Bolan was around somewhere, but in another thirty seconds it would not matter.

"I said get out of the truck, bitch!" Carboni shouted.

The woman, numb from witnessing the cold-blooded murder of her husband, was momentarily frozen in the seat. At Carboni's command, she leaped from the pickup and ran.

As soon as she was away, four rounds of 9 mm parabellums burst through the windshield; one grazed Carboni's shoulder. He started the truck, shifted into low and bombed down the road.

Bolan fisted Big Thunder, aimed and fired.

The .44 round is a .44 revolver bullet mated to a cut-down 7.62mm NATO rifle cartridge case. The AutoMag is as close to a rifle as any handgun can be. Ejected from the 6.5-inch barrel at 1,640 feet per second, the round ripped into the pickup's engine block. It smashed into a piston, ripped the connecting rod away and jammed it into the crankshaft, instantly killing the engine. The pickup wheezed to a stop.

Carboni swore.

As a burst from the Uzi swept into the cab, Carboni slid out the far door and ran for the ditch. His right leg felt as if it was being dipped into fire with every step. His left leg had taken a bullet but did not hurt. He lay in the ditch watching for Bolan. This would be the time! He felt it. He would play dead and let Bolan investigate the pickup—then blow the bastard away and collect the head money. Five million dollars!

He fought off a wave of dizziness and continued to watch the roadway and the pickup.

Five minutes later he was still watching.

A car approached, slowed near the body of Billy Olsen. His widow appeared at the side of the road and flagged it down. She got in and it turned around and raced away.

Carboni knew he had to move. Within minutes the woman would contact the police and the place would soon be swarming with cops.

Move...where? The ditch was too shallow to protect him if he stood, so he crawled away. He saw another farmhouse half a mile away, and recognized it as his best chance. Ahead was a cornfield. Yes! He would run through the corn toward the farm as fast as he could.

He tried to block the pain in his leg and the aches from a dozen bruises and cuts. He was moving, that was the important thing.

To take his mind off the pain of crawling, he concentrated on memories.

He had grown up in a neighborhood in Philly where if you weren't tough you didn't survive.

Kicked out of three high schools, he finally went into business for himself instead of finishing his sophomore year. He became a hubcap specialist for garages, which paid him two dollars a hubcap and sold them for six to twenty. For a year he stole hubcaps on order, making as much as a hundred dollars a week.

Then he got busted and spent six weeks in juvenile detention, where he met guys as tough as he was. On the outside again, he and three of his new friends began a small protection racket.

For six months they prospered. The merchants wanted help controlling the kids on the long block, and if the Pro club told the teen gangs to quit harassing a certain shop, they did or found themselves beaten up.

One shop owner did not understand this form of American free enterprise and refused to pay fifty dollars a week for protection.

Carboni, the biggest of the Pro team, volunteered to have a "talk" with the slender Puerto Rican immigrant who was trying to make a living to support his six children, two sisters, an uncle and three cousins.

The young Carboni called him out in the alley and explained that all the other merchants gladly paid the money to prevent the small gangs of punks from ripping up their stores. The Puerto Rican had learned the money system and could count out change in dollars and cents perfectly, but did not know much English. His fifty English words were not ones Vince Carboni wanted to hear.

Carboni slapped him around a little and the Puerto Rican went for a knife in his pocket. Then Carboni got mad and began to take the "goddamn greaser" apart with his bare hands. The knife got knocked away before it drew blood, and Carboni, who was more than six feet tall and had done enough work in a gym to have developed powerful arms and shoulders, pounded the slender body until it sagged to the ground.

He picked up the unconscious form to give him one last pasting. He swung his big fist at the storekeeper, who was on the verge of consciousness, then swung harder, his scarred knuckles pounding into the man's jaw.

The crack of bones breaking came softly, but Carboni heard them. He left the body in the alley and swaggered away. Damn! He had broken the little guy's neck! He'd killed the son of a bitch!

The police did not interrogate the Pro group. Everyone on the block knew that the Puerto Rican had refused to cooperate, but nobody said a word. Carboni went around to the store owners the next day and signed up six more. They quickly made verbal agreements and turned over two weeks in advance of the new seventy-five-dollar fee.

There was no more trouble with the shop owners for almost a year. Carboni took over the leadership of the Pro team as it moved into burglary and then into the armed robberies of a few liquor stores.

When Carboni held his first .32-caliber revolver, he knew he had found his true calling. He practiced until he was proficient with the little gun, then got a .38 and a year later a World War II .45 automatic, used and battered.

When he was nineteen he was invited to work for a loan shark who occasionally needed "persuasion" power with some of his customers. That marked the beginning of a long and fruitful association with the Mafia and the people who now would pay Carboni five million dollars for the removal of their most persistent threat, Mack Bolan.

Vince Carboni looked up and saw that he had reached the cornfield. He glanced back as he moved up to the side of the road, then peered over the low crown. He could not see the bastard Bolan anywhere. He crawled across the ditch, then rose and ran into the cornfield.

No shots.

He felt better. Now, he wanted to get to the farmhouse, set up a trap for Bolan and collect the five million. He would be a legend in the Mafia, the man who blew away the Executioner!

Fifty yards away, Mack Bolan was tying a makeshift bandage around his upper left arm, which was still bleeding. Although he knew where Carboni was, he had not been in a position to shoot. As he tied the bandage with his right hand and his teeth, he watched Carboni bolt through the corn.

The Executioner frowned as he realized Carboni was heading for another farmhouse. He had to get there first and set up a little surprise for him, a deadly one.

Figuring Carboni would penetrate the field deeply enough to remain hidden, and that that would also mask his view of the road, Bolan rose from the ditch, adjusted his equipment and began a jog along the shoulder. The farmhouse was a little more than half a mile away. He should be there in about three and one-half minutes. Carboni could not make that kind of time through the corn.

Bolan ran up the driveway of the farmhouse and was approaching the back door when a shotgun was pushed through a hole in the screen door, and pointed directly at him. He was no more than ten feet away.

"Don't even breathe hard, young feller. We know all about you. Got it on the telephone. You're the bastard who shot down young Billy Olsen in cold blood. In my time I'd just blast you straight to hell and bury you in the cornfield."

Bolan was staring at the shadowy figure of a man about seventy-five years old. "Sir, you've got the wrong man. I'm chasing the same man you're talking about."

"Not likely. Said you was a good talker. Now put down them weapons and lie down on your back. Do it now. My trigger finger ain't as steady as it used to be."

Bolan's mind raced. Probably buckshot in the gun, which would cut him in two if it hit him. There was nothing nearby to hide behind. There was no bluff left. All he could count on was that the man had slow reflexes.

"I'm not the man you want!" Bolan shouted. "He's coming right down there by your barn." Bolan turned and pointed, dived and rolled the other way, then jumped up and zigzagged behind a picket fence around the inner yard. The shotgun roared, but it was aimed high, probably deliberately. Bolan dashed toward the barn and was soon out of range of the buckshot. No more shots sounded.

Bolan looked at the cornfield. He saw no movement. His gaze swept the area as he would a section of no-man's-land, watching for enemy troop movements. He repeatedly scanned the section nearest the road, moving his eyes like the sweep-line reader on a cathode-ray tube.

He saw a subtle but definite movement of the slender tassels of corn. He watched a wave of motion as though a man was working through the corn toward the barn.

Two cows behind the barn moved slowly into view, chewing their cud. They wandered near the fence toward the spot where the man should emerge from the corn.

Then he appeared. Crouching, Carboni rushed out and ran hard for the barn. The cows were in precisely the wrong spot, shielding Carboni from any shot Bolan could make.

Bolan ran around to the side of the barn and slipped inside. He figured Carboni would come in the building for protection, maybe to pick out an ambush spot. He crouched beside a row of milking stalls and waited.

For a minute there was silence. Then a door squeaked and a shaft of light penetrated the darkness. A silhouette crossed the shaft of light and then the light disappeared as the door closed.

Through the blackness, the Executioner saw that the man whose only job was to kill him stood less than twenty feet away.

Then he heard someone outside the door. Again it opened, again a glaring shaft of light penetrated the blackness, again a dark figure stepped inside and closed the door.

"Now where the hell are you? Seen you come in here, you ornery critter."

It was the old man. Bolan wanted to warn him, but didn't, lest he give away his position. Then the time for warning was gone. Carboni's big .44 AutoMag roared twice. Instantly Bolan raked the area where the AutoMag had fired with a 12-round burst of parabellums.

The back door slid open and before the Executioner could move away from the milking stalls to fire again, Carboni had crawled out. Bolan moved cautiously toward the front of the barn where the old man must be. He opened the door slightly to let in some light and found the farmer on his back, his hands over his chest.

Blood dribbled from his lips.

"I tried to tell you, old-timer," Bolan said gently.

"Oh," the farmer said. "Well, it's too late now." His head turned slowly to one side as his lifeless hand slid to the straw-covered floor.

The Executioner ran to the door. Carboni had killed again, and he was out there somewhere. This was one score the Executioner had to settle now!

13

The Executioner jammed a new magazine in the Uzi and ran to the barn's front door. Outside in the bright afternoon sunshine he saw no movement. The side screen door to the house stood open. He remembered the old man saying "we." Was there a woman in the house?

Then he thought of something more deadly. The farmer had a shotgun; it was likely he also had a rifle. Bolan backed away from the door, realizing that Carboni might already have a rifle from the kitchen or from over the mantel. Found it and be loaded and waiting for Bolan to step out the door.

The Executioner went out the back door and moved around to the side. He could see everything in the yard—the barn, a machine shed, a small granary, a chicken coop, the well house, the house, a garage. Parked in the garage was a Ford Edsel with its unique grill and front end outward. This was one farm that was not entirely up-to-date.

Bolan lay beside the barn, shielded from the house by the foundation. Carboni was not running now. The Executioner could sense the man's hatred, his eagerness to use his long gun.

This would be a battle of willpower and nerves, Bolan decided. He glanced at his watch. Four-thirty. Another three hours until dark. Bolan shifted. He could lie there without moving until dark if he had to, but he knew that Carboni would be active long before that.

Ten minutes later a roar came from an upstairs window. Now a rifle barked six times, as the weapon— a single shot bolt action, Bolan guessed—pounded rounds into each of the buildings the gunner could see from his high ground.

"You son of a bitch! Come out and fight!" Carboni yelled.

Bolan sent five rounds from the Uzi into the open window, then slid back out of sight of the target and waited. After a few moments he moved up quickly, looked at the house, then jerked back as Carboni put a rifle slug into the foundation beside Bolan.

It was a stalemate. Bolan had to turn it around. If he could get close enough he could pitch a fragger in the upstairs window. But by then Carboni might have moved.

He had to lure Carboni out of his shelter and not get himself killed doing it. The Edsel kept creeping into his mind. He ran behind the barn, into the cornfield and over to the rear of the garage. It had a back door. He slipped inside and checked the Edsel. It was out of gas and had one low tire in front.

The machine had not been used for some time.

But Carboni didn't know that. The window where the Mafia hoodlum lay was almost out of sight. Carboni would have to lean out to see the garage. Bolan eased the hand brake off the car, pushed the shift lever to neutral and went to the back of the rig.

The farmyard had a slight slope. Bolan pushed the car to the end of the garage, then jumped back and stayed inside the cover as the Edsel rolled fifty feet forward and stopped. He threw a rock at the Edsel, banging it off the front fender.

Through a crack in one of the boards in the garage Bolan could see the second-floor window. Carboni's head popped out for a second. He looked at the old car and swore.

The Executioner gave the killer enough time to get down the steps and check out the Edsel from a side window in the house. Vince would kill the car or try to get it for his own use.

A minute later the side door jolted open and Carboni ran through it. In each hand he carried a jar with a flaming rag on top of it. A deer rifle was slung over his shoulder. He ran halfway to the car and threw one of the jars. It flew over the Edsel and splattered burning gasoline toward Bolan.

The Executioner blasted four rounds from the Uzi through the smoke. Then he saw the other firebomb sailing through the air and ran to the side. The bomb hit and broke, gushing burning gasoline inside the garage. The Executioner dashed away from the smoke and fire and saw Carboni trying to start the Edsel. The batter ground the starter three times, then the solenoid only clicked as the battery went dead.

Before Bolan could fire, Carboni left the car and ran behind the gasoline smoke screen back into the house.

Slowly the fire ate up the gasoline in the yard. The garage blazed up into a real fire. The Executioner ran to the barn for cover. He waited there for a few moments, then sprinted to the machine shed.

Because Carboni didn't fire again, Bolan figured he must be running short on ammunition for the heavy pistol.

The Executioner looked around. The shed contained a variety of farm implements. Right in front sat a midsize crawler tractor with a bulldozer blade on it. Bolan knew how to operate the machine. He checked the tank; it was half full of diesel fuel. The engine kicked over on the third try, and he lifted the blade until it blocked his view and shielded him from any rifle rounds from Carboni, then nudged the big doors open with the blade.

He hit the throttle and moved straight for the farmhouse's back door. A shot barked from the house, hit the steel dozer blade in front and ricocheted. It sounded like the deer rifle, maybe a 30.06.

The crawler responded well to his touch on the brakes, holding one tread and turning as the other tread kept moving. He adjusted his route once more and clanked, rattled and squeaked straight at the house.

Two more shots came and then silence. Glass broke in an upstairs window. Bolan looked up and realized Carboni could look down past the blade directly at him. He bailed out and ran into the house as a rifle slug from the second floor plowed into the ground where Bolan had been a moment before.

Bolan ran through the kitchen, hunting the stairs. This was house-to-house fighting, something he knew a lot about. He pulled one of the fragger grenades off his combat webbing and held it in his left hand.

The old wooden house creaked as the man upstairs moved around.

The hit man had worked himself into a corner. There was no way he could go except down. Bolan eased halfway up the open stairs and threw the grenade into the room where he figured Carboni was hiding. The bomb went off with a roar.

When the sound echoed across the fields, Bolan listened for human sounds. There were none. He charged up the steps, the Uzi ready with the last rounds in the magazine.

But Carboni was not in the room. Bolan edged around the hall to the second big room, but found it empty, too. The window was open and Bolan watched as Carboni limped across the roof, then ducked and jumped from the low front porch to the ground and out of sight.

Bolan heard a cry of pain as the guy landed on his wounded leg.

For a minute nothing moved. The yard was quiet. Bolan remembered that the hit man did not have the rifle with him when he ran across the roof. He could have dropped it over the side first. Either way the enemy was getting low on ammunition.

Bolan scowled—so was he. There were only five or six rounds in the Uzi, about ten shots left for the big .44 AutoMag, and the Beretta was on its last magazine.

He ran to the other room and looked out at the yard. There was no evidence that Carboni had gone to the barn or any of the sheds. He must still be hugging the first floor of the house. But inside or out?

The garage burned fiercely, sending a trail of black smoke into the sky. Somebody would report it soon by telephone, and a rural fire department would wheel in.

As if responding to his thoughts, a siren wailed in the distance. Bolan snapped a shot from the Beretta into some shadows near the front porch, then pulled back from the window. There was no answering fire.

The siren came closer. Bolan checked both windows again. No Carboni. Where had he gone?

The vehicle with the siren raced down the long farm driveway. That was when Bolan saw that it was a police car or a sheriff's rig. The officer was driving directly into eternity. Carboni would waste him the second he stepped out of his car.

As a warning, the Executioner fired the Uzi near the rig. The car made a fast U-turn and careered toward the barn. When it stopped, the driver darted into the barn.

Now Bolan had another problem. Holding the Uzi in both hands, he ran downstairs and into the kitchen. No sign of Carboni.

At the back door he paused, then jumped on the crawler tractor, started the motor, kicked it into reverse and raced the engine as he let out the clutch and moved to the rear. Bolan was not sure if he took any fire from the front or not, but there had been no shots fired from the barn. He drove the big tractor directly at the open barn door and stopped just before the rear track touched the wood.

In one swift move he leaped off the tractor seat and surged into the barn.

"Don't move," a woman called unsteadily.

The Executioner looked around and saw a uniformed female deputy sheriff holding her service revolver with both hands.

"No problem," Bolan said. "I'm on your side. But we've got a desperate killer out there somewhere. He gunned down the old man who lives here, and I've been trying to dig him out."

The woman frowned. She was young, scared and not sure whether to believe him. Slowly she lowered and then raised the gun.

"How do I know you're not the killer?"

"Would I risk my neck to come back down here and tell you what's going on if I wanted to shoot you?"

She took a deep breath and shook her head, her short hair bouncing under her garrison-style hat.

"No, I guess not."

"Right. I'm Scott, with the FBI. The killer out there is Mafia and he's already murdered three times today. I don't want him to add us to his list."

"What can I do?" Slowly she lowered her gun.

"Get back in your patrol car, sit low in the seat and gun out of here and radio for some more units. We need some help before it gets dark."

"I can do that." Her brown eyes were coming back to normal. A small grin showed. "Hey, I was scared when that round whizzed by the car."

"That was mine. I didn't want you pulling up in front of the house and Carboni blowing your head off."

"Thanks. I better get moving. Where is he, this Carboni?"

"That I would like to know—around the house somewhere."

She nodded, went to the barn door and turned. "Thanks for warning me." She ran to the car and spun gravel off the yard as she powered out of the driveway to the road.

Bolan went to the barn door and stared at the house. A rifle shot splintered the doorframe just over his head. He fell back out of sight and felt a splinter that had gouged his cheek. The shot came from the right side of the house. Almost the same spot where Carboni dropped off the porch. Maybe he had broken an ankle. Or was that too much to hope for?

The Executioner pulled a fragger from his harness and planned his route. His homemade tank was good for attacking, too. He darted out the door to the safety behind the raised blade and fired up the diesel.

He was going blindly now. Then he lowered the blade so he could stand to check his direction. When he was thirty feet from the front corner of the house, he pulled the pin and threw the hand grenade. It went off with a roar, shattering three windows.

Bolan pulled the last fragger from his webbing and powered the tractor forward again, watching alternately ahead and behind, aware that an attack from the rear was a possibility.

The big tractor plowed across the lawn to the front of the house.

The shot came from far to the right, from a field of wheat that was golden brown, dusty dry and ready to cut. The slug broke a window in the house. Bolan stopped the tractor, shut the engine and slipped behind it.

He released the magazine from the Uzi and checked it. There were four rounds left and another in the chamber. Worthwhile taking it along. He had seven rounds left in the Beretta and ten for the .44 AutoMag.

Knowing the extent of his ammo, the Executioner ran around the tractor and headed toward Carboni.

A slight wind picked up as he ran into the field. The weather was warm and dry. With every step Bolan mashed down wheat, but there was no other way. He saw Carboni running to the left and followed in that direction. Had the hit man given up on his target or was he luring Bolan into some kind of a trap?

If it was a trap, it had to be a good one. Bolan had no idea how the Mafia goon could set up anything out here.

From the gait of the man ahead of him, Bolan knew he was wounded worse than before. One of the parabellums must have hit flesh.

Bolan ran faster, his own arm wound almost forgotten as he held the Uzi. It was his long-range try. If that failed he would discard the heavy weapon and move in with his pair of handguns.

The wind increased, and Bolan wondered if there was going to be a late-afternoon thunderstorm. His watch showed 5:15. Lots of time before dark. He saw clouds scudding with the strong winds.

The Executioner came over a small rise in the wheat field and looked for his target. The man was not in sight. Bolan stopped running and scanned the general area where he had last seen Carboni. The wheat came nearly to Bolan's waist. Carboni could be down somewhere in the eighty-acre field, out of sight and crawling toward a ditch.

The wind blew stronger in Bolan's face and he wished he could smell out his enemy. Ahead he saw the grain waver and tremble in one spot. He sent two rounds from the Uzi there and waited.

Nothing.

He scanned the northern part of the field again.

Lightning flashed a dozen miles away, and the roll of thunder came faintly.

Momentarily standing above the wheat, Carboni saw Bolan and dived again. Bolan saw him and surged toward him through the high wheat until he felt as if he were running through water.

He was close now to Carboni, and had out the big .44 AutoMag, watching and waiting.

The wisp of smoke rose to his left, then another rose in front of him, and in five seconds a solid wall of flame was consuming the stalks. The wind whipped the fire into a frenzy. Almost at once the flames were eight feet high and roaring toward Bolan.

The Executioner turned, but suddenly flames appeared ahead of him. He turned again—more fire.

He was surrounded by fire.

He heard a weird, wild laugh from Carboni, who stood on the already burned and blackened stalks, screaming in delight.

Bolan wanted to run, to leap through the flames. He could pull his shirt over his face and hair. The flames roared closer. His small island of unburned wheat was shrinking drastically.

The Executioner heard the crazed laugh again as he prepared for his dash. There was no guarantee that he would make it. The ravaging fire would suck up all of the oxygen in the air. He must try to hold his breath until he was out of the flames.

The wild laugh came once more and Bolan unleashed two shots from the .44 AutoMag in that direction, then held the big gun and backed up six feet to make his dash.

He was ready. Was this the way he was going to buy the farm? If it happened, it happened. He began to run.

As he moved the wind shifted, and he stopped, unsure what effect it would have on the flames. The fickle wind changed again, now blowing in the opposite direction.

Lightning split the cloudy sky, hitting a tree about half a mile away.

The flames ahead of him died down for lack of fuel, blowing back on the blackened wasteland. The fire behind him raced forward, but all he had to do now was jump over the crawling, low flames to the smoking ashes of the ruined wheat field.

Carboni's wild laughter had turned to screams of terror. Bolan saw him ahead, charging around in the middle of a circle of fire. Carboni was trapped.

Lightning struck the ground a hundred yards away and the smell of raw sulfur blended with the smoke. Bolan jolted into action. He ran through the burned area, getting safely away from the flames.

When he looked back at the spot where he had last seen Carboni, he could see only the flames whipping forward, consuming the entire circle that had protected the Mafia hit man. It had developed into a searing, boiling fire storm.

Bolan knew he should wait for the fire to burn out and check for a body to be sure that Vince Carboni was dead. But an inner voice drew him away.

He figured Carboni had had only a small chance of escaping the flames.

Now Bolan had to return to his contacts in the police department and talk to Nino Tattaglia in the Mafia snakepit to find out if the schedule was holding. He had to know for sure if the "changes" in the police department were still set for tomorrow night.

For a moment he wondered if he could trust Assistant Chief Jansen. He could have set up that "blackmail" situation for Bolan's benefit. For now Bolan would trust only his own instincts and make everyone else prove himself.

Immediately he had the problem of getting back to town. He discarded the Uzi in the wheat field. It had been a gift from the Mafia. He threw away his combat webbing and web belt. He had extras in his hotel.

He hid his two handguns in his shirt as he jogged to the closest highway, then hitchhiked into the nearest town where he could find a taxi.

The thought still plagued him—could he entirely trust Chief Jansen, or did Jansen have his eye on the top spot as chief of police working with the Mafia?

14

The phone rang five times before Assistant Chief Jansen picked it up. He had been sleeping soundly.

"Yeah, I'm here. What time is it?" He looked at the clock on his nightstand. "Two-thirty! Who the hell is this?"

"I'm your blood brother, Jansen. You remember the motel. I've been busy today. Anything new going down on the new police policies?"

"Not that I could see. There was a fire in Gwynns Falls Park. Looks like Captain Davis met hell a little early. I figured you might have made the introduction. That's been put down as an accident. Any comment?"

"He must have deserved it. Anything doing with the other two assistant chiefs?"

"Not a thing. They're sitting tight, doing what they have to do but really marking time. One of them took the day off today."

"Has Chief Smith showed up yet?"

"No. You said he wasn't hurt? There's a lot of speculation downtown about him. The police commissioner is furious."

"Smith must be lying low for a day or two. Anybody else bother you?"

"No. Not a problem. I heard there was a shootout north of town today. You involved in that one?"

"For a while. Personal matter. Will you be at the mayor's State of the City talk tomorrow night?"

"Plan to be. I'm part of the official delegation from the department."

"Good. I'll talk to you tomorrow. Have a nice sleep."

Bolan hung up and considered calling Tattaglia, but decided to wait. He could use a few hours of sleep himself. His left arm began to throb again. He put an antiseptic, antibiotic salve and a bandage on the wound. It would heal but leave a scar. He really did not need another one.

Ten minutes later he was asleep.

The next morning at seven, Bolan called Tattaglia.

"Who the hell is calling in the middle of the night?"

"Morning, Nino. Greetings from Leo. Any developments?"

"Oh, it's you. Quiet yesterday. Probably before some kind of a storm. They don't tell me much yet. But it's tonight."

"Right, at the mayor's bash. I'll be there. Heard anything about the chief?"

"Heard something about a chief once or twice, but I'm not high enough up the totem pole."

"Get up there. We need you."

"Working on it."

"Leo will encourage you. Remember, he can yank you back to that cell anytime he wants."

"I know it. I'm cooperating."

"Keep your eyes open, and be sure you're packing tonight. You have a legal concealed-weapons permit, don't you?"

"Yes."

"Stay hard."

Bolan hung up and checked the name of a lawyer he had to see. The man should be in his office by nine.

The Executioner was sitting in the lawyer's big swivel chair when the barrister came in that morning. No one else was in the office.

"Good morning, Payne Sanders. Sit down and let's talk."

"Who the hell are you? Get out of my chair and out of my office or I'll call the security guard."

Bolan stood over the five-foot-ten lawyer. Icy blue eyes bored into Payne's. The smaller man stepped back.

"You touch me and I'll sue you for assault and battery." Sanders said it evenly, but the punch had gone out of his voice. He retreated another step.

"Stay here, Sanders. We have to talk. Sit down and make yourself comfortable."

He wiped his sweaty forehead and sat in the client's chair beside his desk, where he almost never sat.

"I understand you were legal counsel for Capt. Harley Davis. He left certain documents with you that were to be turned over to the police in the event of his untimely death. I'm here to pick them up."

"I had no connection with any Harley Davis. I am certainly not his lawyer."

Bolan sighed and rose. He stepped to the chair and stared down at the lawyer.

"Mr. Sanders, I'm hoping that such an obvious lie doesn't mean that you've already disposed of the documents to a higher bidder. I know the Mafia don, Carlo Nazarione, would pay plenty to have those papers and pictures. Have they thought to contact you about them yet?"

"No. They haven't contacted me because I have nothing they might want—certainly nothing involving Mr. Davis, whoever he is."

"Good try, Sanders. Acting class was obviously your best subject. Don't try it again. I don't have a lot of time." Bolan took a five-inch knife from the sheath inside his boot. The narrow finely-honed blade glistened in the brightly lit office.

"Sanders, I once read an FBI seminar brochure that said it is not productive to try to encourage a person to give out information by what they called digital trauma. You can figure out what that means."

Sanders shrank in his chair. "If I knew this Davis, I'd be glad to cooperate."

"I don't agree with the FBI. Putting fingers out of joint can be a fine way to encourage a man to talk."

Sweat appeared on Sanders's forehead.

"What was the name again?"

"Capt. Harley Davis of the Baltimore Police Department."

"My secretary takes care of all of those 'in case of' files. Let me contact her and see."

Bolan shook his head. He touched the tip of the knife to the lawyer's shoulder.

"No way. That valuable file is right here in your office. All you have to do is stand up, get the file and hand it to me. How much did Nazarione offer you for it?"

"A hundred thousand. I'm a businessman."

"And you told him two hundred thousand and he dickered and you hung up."

"Something like that."

"You're a brave man, Sanders. I've known Mafia dons who would have you turned into turkey meat for a cute trick like that. You're also lucky. I'd say a week in the Caribbean should put you in the clear. Baltimore is going to be extremely unhealthy for you for the next week."

"I was just trying to make a couple of dollars!" Sanders was blinking back the tears.

"They would kill you right now if they knew how to get the documents and photos. I'm going to turn them over to the police, so let's have them right now."

Sanders put his head in his hands and cried. He looked up, tears on his cheeks. "He suckered me into it three years ago. I have lots of 'in case of death open and deliver' files. But this one kept growing and growing. It was sealed, but I opened it and made copies. Man, he certainly had the goods on these Mafia goons! He could nail them to the wall anytime he wanted. I knew they were paying him off.

"The problem was they wouldn't pay me off for the same material. I jacked up my price to Davis a little and he never even noticed. The file got so thick I stopped looking in it. When he died, I didn't know what to do. Being an officer of the court I was honor bound to turn over evidence to the court, the D.A., the police. But I held off. Then Nazarione himself called me. We met and talked. He gave me a packet of twenty one-hundred-dollar bills as a tip. Said there was lots more."

"Nazarione needs those papers," Bolan said.

"Last night he called me at home. Asked about my three kids and my wife, and while there was no threat, I certainly got the idea they might not be safe if I didn't do what he said."

"The files, Sanders. Get them now. Nazarione will probably be here this morning with a wrecking bar to take your office apart."

Sanders stood up like an old man. He was about forty. He went to a wall safe and spun the dials. When it was unlocked, Bolan eased the lawyer aside and opened it. Inside was a .38 revolver. Bolan took it out, then let Sanders reach in. He brought out two cardboard boxes.

"I could copy everything and give you the originals and give the copies to Nazarione...."

Bolan shook his head. "No time. Anyway, he would check for that." The Executioner opened the first letter-size cardboard file and leafed through some of the papers and pictures. It was hard evidence. He closed the file and picked up both boxes.

"I suggest you call your wife and meet her and the kids away from your home. Then drive to Washington and take the first flight to Nassau. You deserve a vacation."

Bolan carried the two boxes out of the office and took the stairs down the five flights to the street. He met no one coming up.

A mile away from the building, he stopped at a telephone booth and called Assistant Chief Jansen.

"This is your bloody buddy. Has the chief turned up yet?"

"No. We're worried here. His wife hasn't heard from him for two days."

"Forget him—he's dead, captured or scared. I have something you need for the show tonight. Meet me in twenty minutes in that McDonald's just down from your headquarters. Alone, right?"

"You got it. The other two assistant chiefs are starting to show their muscle around here."

"They won't after tonight. Anything on Assistant Chief Vincent?"

"We've put his arraignment off until next week. I had a talk with the D.A., explaining what I think happened. I said things should be more clear after tonight. We might be able to withdraw the charges and get him back on duty yet."

"Good. Twenty minutes."

Bolan was there in five and watched from an inside booth. He saw no sudden influx of male civilians, no prowling unmarked police cars. Jansen was keeping his word.

The chief came in five minutes later, bought a milk shake at the counter and looked for a place to sit. He saw Bolan, walked up and sat across from him. They greeted each other.

"What's the procedure tonight with the mayor?" Bolan asked.

"Usually he presents his speech for the audience and the TV cameras and then an open city-council meeting begins."

"How does your police commissioner fit in?"

"He's the politics end. He works with the mayor and gives directions to our chief, who implements them through the department."

"So the commissioner and the mayor make the policy and the rest of you carry it out."

"Right."

The Executioner lifted a file folder from one of the boxes beside him and slid it across the table to Jansen.

"Here's the file that shows and proves the Mafia's penetration into the Baltimore Police Department, including the two assistant chiefs. Here's a list of who is on the take and why. There is also a complete rundown of some ten or twelve top-echelon Mafia types with names and dates and evidence to back up killings, briberies, assaults and a dozen other crimes never charged against them before."

He let Jansen look through the file.

"This is a bombshell! It will blow the department wide open!"

"Not if the district attorney goes at it slowly and the department does a lot of internal housecleaning. I was hoping we could set off the first bomb tonight with the mayor's speech."

"He's probably still writing it," Jansen said.

"Good. Maybe we have time. First, make copies of everything in these files. Then take the originals to the D.A. and explain the whole thing. Then take some select items to the police commissioner and see if he can get something in the mayor's speech about law enforcement, the new crackdown on the Mafia, and mention a couple of cases. It might work. I didn't see any mention of Police Commissioner Williams in any of the material. He must be clean."

"Yes. The D.A. will go along with almost anything to get this evidence. Is this what Captain Davis had that he was blackmailing Nazarione with?"

"Yes, I got it from Davis's lawyer, but he will never admit that. It's found evidence. Maybe you could suggest to the D.A. that they prepare arrest warrants for the two assistant chiefs on bribery and four or five Mafia hoods on some of the cases covered in the files. If the mayor could announce those arrests and have the men picked up at the gathering, it would be a big political boost for him."

"And the start of our cleanup. I'll give it a try. The D.A. will go along. I just hope I can convince Commissioner Williams. I've never been one of his favorites."

"You will be after you show him all that evidence and tell him it's been turned over to the D.A. He won't be able to stop it then if he is working with Nazarione."

Chief Jansen finished his milk shake. "Anything on Chief Smith?"

"Not a word. Hasn't he reported in yet?"

"Not so far. Maybe the Mafia found him at that motel where you left him."

"Possible. Get things in motion. We don't have much time."

Chief Jansen nodded, left the booth and walked out the side door.

FIFTY MILES NORTH of Baltimore, Chief of Police Smith paced the small motel room. He was unshaven and wore only his T-shirt and pants. For the third time he ran out of cigarettes. He crushed the pack and threw it against the wall.

What the hell was he supposed to do? He had tried to get through on the phone but they said not to call, to wait until after tonight.

This was the mayor's big State of the City speech. He usually helped the commissioner put together something complimentary the mayor could say about the department, some new record of arrests or how crime was down in certain sections.

Maybe he should give the commissioner a call?

And how would he explain where he had been for the past two or three days?

He thought back to the day when he had been on his way home and had seen the crew wagon boiling up behind. He knew what to expect—he was on the floor of the side-armored police car long before his driver had shouted.

Then damn Bolan had interfered at the last minute and riddled those Mafia goons. There was nothing to do then but go along with the Executioner and his rescue. But what did Carlo Nazarione think about eleven of his men getting killed on what was supposed to be a simple kill of the driver and kidnapping of the chief?

Evidently he was damn mad.

Chief Smith put on shoes, socks and shirt. He had to get out of there and do some tall thinking.

15

Cheers came from all sides. The city was in the best financial condition it had been in years. There was money to provide more family services to the needy and unemployed. There were more people with jobs than ever before.

The mayor turned it on for all it was worth and his political appointees and loyal party members, all carefully selected for the choice seats in the hall, responded appropriately.

"One more term! One more term! One more term!" the faithful chanted.

The mayor grinned. He had the best political smile in the state. Next he wanted the governor's chair, then either the Senate or the White House.

The mayor paused. "Our great police department has been making rapid strides, as well. Less than half an hour ago our police detectives moved in with arrest warrants on six people in our community who some of you may still think are model citizens. In reality these six are members of the international organized-crime group known as the Mafia. They include Carlo Nazarione, the Baltimore godfather, and Nino Tattaglia, as well as Ardly Scimone.

"These men will be given a speedy trial, along with three others, as specified under law.

"It does pain me to reveal that one of those arrested is one of our assistant chiefs, Booker T. Edwards. Chief Edwards has been put on leave pending his trial. He has been charged with accepting a bribe and failure to report such a happening.

"Police Commissioner Williams has assured me that any police officer who accepts a 'gratuity' will be quickly routed out and prosecuted. The commissioner also has reported to me that Chief of Police Smith is currently missing. He has not been seen by the department or his family for three days. I am therefore appointing as temporary chief of police Larry Jansen.

"In closing, I'd like to remind you of the many glorious achievements of this administration, and to show you that we are in this fight to rid our city of the Mafia. We do not cover up. We could have 'retired' Chief Edwards, swept it all under the rug. We did not. We will not. Bad cops are going to jail. Now could I ask you to do something for me? What was that chant I heard that I liked so much a few minutes ago?"

The crowd responded with another two minutes of "One more term!" with shouting and clapping in unison.

Mack Bolan stood beside the speaker's stand. He had arrived with Chief Jansen and been given a VIP badge. Jansen was beside the mayor as he left the stand. Bolan moved in behind them.

"Jansen, I don't ever want you to do that again. No more going over my head to the D.A. Goddamn it, I should have seen all of that material before you showed it to him! I might have wanted to save Edwards. He was the only black we had as assistant chief. Yeah, sure Police Commissioner Williams is black, but so is most of our town. We need more black sergeants and captains. Get them. Fix the test scores if you have to, but I want more blacks in the top echelons of your department. And dig up Chief Smith. Put six detectives on finding him. I want to know what he thinks he's doing.''

"Yes, sir, your honor. We'll get right on it. And we're going to be prosecuting these Mafia goons as fast as we can.''

Jansen was sweating when he turned and motioned to Bolan. They went out a side door. When they were outside alone Jansen said, "Is it always this hot at the top?''

"You haven't even started to feel the heat yet. Wait until you blow out that second assistant chief.''

"Yeah, and I have to find some black captains and sergeants in a hurry.''

"I've got another problem for you. I didn't see that evidence on Tattaglia. You need to make a phone call.''

"About Tattaglia? We've got him good.''

They drove to a pay phone where Bolan dialed a number, and when someone answered he grinned.

"Hope I got you away from a fantastic dinner party,'' the Executioner said.

"No chance, cowboy. Know that voice anywhere. What's happening?''

"Want you to talk to a friend of mine, Chief Jansen of the Baltimore Police. Tell him about Nino.''

"Easy. Put him on.''

Bolan looked at Jansen. "This man is Phillip Hardesty of the federal Department of Justice. He wants to talk to you."

Jansen took the phone.

"Mr. Hardesty, is there something I should know about Nino Tattaglia?"

"Yes indeed, chief. Nino is ours. He was Mafia and we turned him around to take my place as our high-level informant. You can pick him up and hold him for a couple of days, but then the evidence against him has to be compromised or lost. He won't do us any good rotting in a Maryland jail somewhere."

"This is news to me. Your friend isn't overly talkative."

"Neither one of them is supposed to be. I'll send you a letter through channels, and I want you to call the department tomorrow and double-check that I'm who I say I am. We need Nino right where he is, and higher up in the mob. I'm sure you'll cooperate."

"Yes. I guess all this evidence against the Mafia is ours partly because of Nino's work with your tall friend here."

"Affirmative."

"Okay, it can be arranged. We'll push other cases, drag this for a week and let him go without any formal charges. Mr. Hardesty, we thank you for your help."

"Just doing my job. Put Mack back on."

Bolan took the phone.

"Yeah, Leo?"

"Leo's dead, didn't you hear? Went to Italy on vacation and died in a fiery car crash."

"May he rest in peace. So now Leo is off the Mafia hook."

"Completely off. How's Nino doing?"

"Fair. He forgets sometimes. You better give him a couple of reminders."

"I'll do that. Take care."

They hung up.

Chief Jansen frowned. "Who the hell am I going to move up to captain?" He shook his head. "Up to now I've only been working fourteen hours a day. From now on it will be twenty-four hours on, zero off."

"I'm crying for you," Bolan said, grinning. "You love it. I'll let you get back to work. I have a few loose ends to take care of. I'll give you a call tomorrow."

They waved and went their separate ways. He was sure now that Chief Jansen was clean. Otherwise he never would have told him about Nino.

CHIEF SMITH HAD TOUCHED his own private panic button. When he got the rental car that first day he had driven fifty miles north of Baltimore. That put him on the outskirts of York, Pennsylvania. He took a motel room there and tried to call Nazarione. No one there would talk to him. They simply asked where he was, but he would not tell them.

He had walked around town most of the day, trying to decide what to do. Now he knew. He had to return to Baltimore, go to the big house and talk with Carlo. Almost any problem could be worked out face-to-face.

It was dark now, and he remembered this was the day of the mayor's State of the City speech. He wondered how it went. He would hear some of it on the evening news. But he could not find a good news station on the car radio.

Just after ten that evening he arrived at the front gate of Nazarione's mansion, told the guard his name and requested to see the capo. It was an emergency. The sentry went into the gate house and used the telephone. He emerged a minute later, nodded and opened the heavy gate by pushing a button. Electric motors rolled the steel framework to one side.

"Mr. Nazarione said you should come right up to the house. Leave the car in the lower parking lot and go to the front door."

"Thank you," Smith said. Some of his old confidence was coming back. Things were not as bad as he thought or Carlo never would have let him in. The guard did not even search him.

He swept up the curving, beautifully landscaped drive and turned into the lower parking lot, which was about fifty yards from the front door and the small upper parking lot.

Chief Smith locked the far door, got out of the car, locked the driver's side and was about ready to pocket the keys when he felt someone touch his shoulder.

Smith snapped around, surprised, startled. Behind him was a man almost six and a half feet tall, with a hulking kind of brutish body that he had grown to recognize over the years. An enforcer!

"I'm Chief Smith. Mr. Nazarione said I was to come up to the front door and then see him."

His confidence slipped when the huge man grinned.

"Yeah, that's what the man told you. He told me something different."

The big man swung a huge fist. Chief Smith saw it coming, wanted to move out of the way but couldn't. The heavy knuckles slammed into the side of his face. His head snapped back and his glasses flew off. Then he saw another fist coming; it jolted into his right eye, and the world became dark and dull. Soon something else hit his face, and the whole scene wavered and switched from dark to deep black.

Chief Smith felt something touch him. It was soft, then sharp and pointed and piercing his skin.

"He's coming around," a voice from the blackness said.

"No damn fun if he don't!"

"Smith, you bastard, wake up."

Strong hands pulled him to a sitting position, and he nearly tipped over. He struggled to open his eyes. They refused. A sharp slap on the face brought him from dreamland.

He sat on a rough wooden floor. The room was chilly. He was in a circle of light with nothing but blackness beyond.

"Well, look who's here—our wonderful chief of police, that bastard Smith." The voice was harsh, irritating, frightening. Smith tried to remember where he had heard it before. No luck.

He blinked. This was not right. Carlo had sounded friendly.

"I'm not supposed to be here. Didn't Carlo tell you guys? I'm on your side. I have been for two months now. Tell Carlo that I'm here, would you please?"

"Carlo ain't here."

"We're wasting time," a third voice said.

"We got all night."

The third voice argued. "You might have all night, but I don't and neither does the machine. I have to start it in just under ten minutes so it can finish by 4:30 A.M. when the first trucks come."

"Yeah, hell, okay."

A small penknife sliced through the air and hit Smith over his kidney. He swore softly, dived to the floor and doubled his legs up to his chest, then turned and threw up.

"Guy can't hold his lunch, let alone his booze."

A bucket of ice water sloshed over the writhing form. Smith stopped retching and shivered.

"Strip," one voice told him. Smith kept shivering on the floor. The iron tip of a cattle prod, wired for electricity, touched his bare neck. Smith stiffened and vibrated like an automatic cement finisher.

"This guy has no staying power at all," a voice said.

"Hell, no. Remember that guy who took over a hundred jolts before he finally passed out? This sucker ain't good for more than two or three."

"Get his clothes off," the impatient voice demanded.

Hands reached in and jerked at buttons, belt and shoes. Two minutes later Smith lay naked on the wet planking, the intense stream lights still blasting into his eyes every time he looked up.

The cattle prod touched Smith's scrotum and he screamed in pain as the electricity jolted through his genitals.

"Damn, but he's sensitive. Smith, you bastard. Stand up and hold out your left arm, or you get the cattle prod again."

Smith stared in the direction of the speaker. Then he stood and held out his arm.

A baseball bat swung down sharply against the white, hairless forearm. The crack of bones breaking came almost instantaneously. Smith roared in pain and terror as he dropped to his knees, cradling his broken arm against his stomach. His scream ended but the pain remained and he swore again and again.

"Now we're getting somewhere," a different voice said.

"Smith, you bastard. This is just a sample of what happens to guys who double-cross the family and Carlo Nazarione. They get pounded around."

Another bucket of ice-cold water sloshed over Smith and his whole body shivered and shook.

"I worked with you guys. I never... never finked out!"

"What about those dozen guys you got slaughtered on that simple little pickup job?"

"I explained that to Carlo. I never knew this Bolan character was around. So he rescued me. Why didn't you let us go? I would have been at Carlo's gate half an hour later."

The cattle prod touched Smith and he jerked away but it followed. Then he attempted to hold out through the shock waves, but at last screamed and fell to the floor on his back, protecting his broken arm.

"We're wasting time," the heavy voice said again.

"Yeah, sure. But he has to know. He has to know why."

"I didn't do nothing! I was coming over on your side. Why do you suppose I been getting all those Mafia guys off on easy plea bargaining?"

"Sure, and then you sell us out, bring in the Executioner, and the bastard rips us to shreds!"

"So now he knows. We've got four minutes."

"Okay, okay." One of the men in the shadows took out a knife and threw it. The five-inch blade plunged deeply into Smith's bare thigh. He shrieked with pain, but before he could remove the knife, a dark blur jumped into the light, pulled out the blade and returned to the shadows.

Smith looked up, his pain etching a grotesque mask on his face, then passed out.

"Just as well," a voice said. "Help me get him over there."

Three men lugged the unconscious form to the side of a large metal tank, and laid him in a metal box five feet long, eighteen inches wide and two feet high, one of sixty such boxes in the huge tank.

"Hell, play your games," one of the voices said.

The man who had been rushing everyone pushed two buttons on a panel, then two more and the metal forms inside the big tank began to move slowly forward.

The boxes were in three rows, each twenty boxes long. The first three came to a series of high-pressure nozzles. A finger touched a button and chilled water gushed from the nozzles into the containers. They filled and the next three empty tanks moved into place.

The casket-shaped box containing Chief Smith was next in line. He came to as the container ahead was filling with water.

One of the men took out his .45 but the others shook their heads. The cattle prod touched Smith's bare shoulder and he pulled away, bellowing in pain and anger.

Then he saw the nozzles and the water surging into the tank ahead of him.

He tried to stand. A baseball bat swung around and slammed into his back. He slumped into the box. He tried to crawl out, but the cattle prod and the bat touched him again and again.

Chief Smith screamed as his container moved forward on the cog machinery and the heavy chain. When the first splashes of water hit him he realized what was happening.

"I got a wife and three kids! You don't want to do this. You scared me, you hurt me. I've learned my lesson. Let me out. For God's sake, let me out of here!"

The water chilled him immediately, making his legs useless. He lifted his good arm and the ball bat swung, breaking the bone.

Chief Smith stared at the men. Someone had turned on the lights and he could see them now. There were two Mafia thugs and a smaller man in a white shirt and tie, probably the manager of this plant. He knew at once what it was, but he couldn't believe what was happening.

"You can't do this! Call Carlo, he'll tell you I been cooperating great for six months now, and nobody knew. Not even that slime Captain Davis."

The chief's voice went high then, as the ice-cold water covered his legs and worked up his torso. His heart was pumping wildly to bring warm blood to the frigid areas.

The water rose to his chest, four inches from the top of the container. Automatically the weight of the box tripped the off switch and the container moved ahead.

Chief Smith looked forward and screamed. His head was above water, and over the top of the metal container. Two feet down the chain the boxes passed through an opening barely large enough to let them slip inside. There was only two inches leeway into the freezer box, where the containers would "cook" for eight hours to turn them into five-foot blocks of crystal-clear ice.

Chief Smith's screams were endless. Both of the Mafia men laughed, making a bet on whether he would or would not pass out again before entering the freezer.

The container behind his was full and began to move slowly forward.

Chief Smith looked at the sheer side of the heavy metal opening ahead. He had to lower his shoulders and head or be decapitated. Slowly he sank into the water, immersing his shoulders, neck, chin, mouth. The water was now within an inch of the top of the container. Expansion would move it up to the top. Now he had two inches between his nose, the water and the oncoming top of the freezer.

His head moved yet lower.

Then he relaxed and smiled. Hell, he was in his own swimming pool and diving for marbles on the bottom with the kids. Damn, they were good! He took a deep breath and headed for the bottom, wondering why his arms would not work. It was going to be a great day of swimming with the kids. Hell, he'd taken the day off from work. That was why they built the pool!

The two Mafia killers stared in amazement.

"See that? He just went under, no scream, no getting his head chopped off."

"Must have been out of his skull. Hey, think of the big surprise some ice man is going to have tomorrow when he starts taking the big slabs of ice out. Inside one of them there will be the former chief of police. Bet you fifty bucks that asshole Smith will even have a smile frozen on his face."

"No bet. Give the man the five hundred and let's get out of here."

"Five hundred? I thought this was Carlo's ice house."

The taller hit man shook his head.

The other one went to talk to the plant operator.

"All automatic, right?" the Mafia goon asked.

"Yeah, right. I pushed the buttons. It will fill the cubes, feed them into the freezing area and even turn out the lights in this section."

"Good," the hit man said. "That makes it easier." He shot the operator twice in the face, made sure he was dead, then left for the car.

"You didn't think we could leave a witness who wasn't in the family to a kill like that, did you?" the hit man asked. He split the five hundred with his partner. They went to the car and drove away.

16

The form huddled on the dark Maryland ground did not move. When the sudden coolness of the thundershower erupted over the land, the body twitched, writhed, then returned to consciousness.

Vince Carboni sat up in the rain-drenched wheat field. He lowered his hands to support himself. When they touched the ground he cried out in terrible, agonizing pain.

Carboni looked at his hands and saw the charred flesh. Sweat beaded on his forehead.

Damned near burned to death, he thought as he looked around. It was dark. The hard shower was a quick one, soaking him thoroughly, dumping an inch of water on the land in fifteen minutes, then charging away.

He could not move his fingers. His arms were hairless, black in spots with heavy burns. His pants had burned halfway to his knees, and he wondered if he could walk on his blackened legs.

Carboni remembered that the wind had shifted suddenly and blown the wall of fire toward him, cutting off his escape route. The flames had danced all around him like a fire storm. He had tried to run through the fire, but the flames had been so intense he could not breathe.

Now he took a deep breath and screamed. A new pain seared inside him. His lungs must be scorched, too.

Move. He had to move or die. He had to get to a doctor or a hospital or he might not even live until morning. His head felt strangely cool.

His hair!

It had burned off. He felt damned lucky to be alive. Vaguely he remembered crawling from the blackened stalks into this unburned part. Or was it across a road?

Road.

The word touched his logic center. He should move toward the road. Where was it?

He heard something disturb the stillness of the countryside. It sounded again, closer. He looked and saw lights—headlights! The road was that way, and not far. He tried to stand. He cried out in pain when he pressed down with his hands to rise.

Slowly he moved to his knees and balanced there a moment before he attempted to straighten up.

Three times he tried. Three times he fell. On the fourth try he windmilled his arms and gained his balance.

But could he walk? He tried one short step and did not fall. Took a second step, then a third. He turned toward the road. The car had long since passed. He had no way of knowing how far away the road was, but even a hundred yards would be a marathon for him.

His feet were not burned inside the shoes. That might be all that saved his life . . . if he could get to the road.

Another car came, and he saw he was now less than a hundred feet from the road, but he would not get there in time to stop the car.

One more step.

Another step.

He felt as if he were walking through knee-deep mud. He had never been so tired, so physically spent.

"Lucky to be alive. Lucky to be alive!" He chanted the words out loud as he worked with half steps slowly toward the hazy shape of the ditch ahead and the road.

Damn, it was a long way.

For the first time in years he had not checked to see if his weapon was in place. Now his clublike hands reached for his hip holster. It was empty, the big .44 AutoMag gone. Should not have a holster on. People would ask questions.

He tried to undo it. His belt went through a loop on his holster; again and again he tried to get the belt unfastened. His hands refused to obey his commands. Three fingers on his right hand were burned together.

Carboni tried with his left hand. On the fourth try he opened the belt and painfully pulled it out of the loops until the holster fell off.

He took a deep breath of relief, only to scream as the cool air hit his burned lungs. He gagged, almost threw up, then shook his head in fury and frustration and continued for the road.

He realized his shirt was nearly burned off. There was little left of the front. He would need a great story to explain this. He would think of something. First, the road.

He struggled ahead.

The ditch itself came as a surprise. He fell into it and rolled into the foot of water from the thunderstorm. The coolness felt marvelous on his burning hands. He immersed them again, then dunked his head.

He almost lapsed into unconsciousness. The sound of a car whizzing by roused him. He struggled to his hands and knees. His hands felt better. He turned his palms upward, raised his fingers and used the backs of his wrists to hold his weight as he crawled forward.

He lay at the edge of the blacktopped lane, hoping the next driver saw him before he ran over him.

Vince Carboni, who vowed to destroy Mack Bolan, lay on the warm blacktop waiting to find out if he would live or die.

MACK BOLAN DROVE BACK to his hotel and changed from a conservative business suit to a black skin suit with the silenced Beretta 93-R under his arm. He hooked a fragger on his web belt opposite his "flesh-shredding" .44 AutoMag.

He called Nino Tattaglia but there was no answer. He probably had already been picked up by the police. This would help cement his position in the mob, and he would be out in a week or so.

Bolan figured Nazarione would find out about the warrants for him before they could be served. Which meant he would be holed up in his mansion or off on a sudden trip in his private jet. Either way there was one proved method to find out.

Wearing a light-blue jacket to cover his weapons, the Executioner went to the rented car and drove to the Nazarione estate.

He parked within a block of the gate and left his car unlocked in case a quick getaway would be needed. He walked to the high block wall bordering the estate, seeing that only the second floor of the mansion was lit. He slipped along the wall to a point across from the pool and its acre of lawn. This was the long way to the house. It also should be the least patrolled.

Bolan peered over the wall. Security seemed nonexistent. Perhaps Nazarione was trying to convince prospective jurors that he was just another businessman. A guard slid from a shadowy area beside the pool to some low trees and worked toward the fence. He made a circuit of the fence, then passed behind the house. Only one guard outside?

Again he studied the house. Rooms were lit on the second floor, but no lights showed on the first or third floors or in the half basement recreation and crew rooms he had seen before.

Possum. They were playing possum, pretending not to be there. The Executioner would find out in a hell of a rush. He took the small radio detonator from his pocket and flipped the toggle switch to activate it, then pushed the red button twice.

There was an immediate splintering roar from one of the bombs Bolan had planted days before in the mansion. The first came from the third floor, the one near Nazarione's office. Almost at once a deeper, heavier roar came from the half basement; that would be the powder magazine and arms cache. Two more smaller blasts added to the noises echoing in the previously quiet neighborhood.

No fire was visible. Dust spewed from upper windows, and clouds of smoke and dust gushed from the basement door.

Calling to somebody, the guard ran for the basement. Bolan scaled the wall, darted for the shadows, then worked across the lawn to the back door. It was unlocked. He cautiously slid inside. He expected at least five hardmen guarding the don. There did not seem to be that many.

A shout sounded above. A door opened near Bolan. It was the elevator. A tall man ran out, a handkerchief held to the side of his head, a .45 in his right hand. He saw Bolan and fired, but too late—his target had leaped into the shelter of a doorway. Bolan returned the fire with the Beretta on single shot.

The man was Nazarione. He ran out the door and into the yard.

Bolan waited to see that no one was backing him, then raced after the Mafia don. He met a hardman rounding the corner of the hall. The Executioner stroked the trigger of the Beretta automatically, putting two rounds in the Mafia soldier's chest, eliminating him from the payroll for all time.

The Executioner charged the side door. By the time he was outside he heard a car engine roar, and reached the parking lot in time to see a crew wagon race away.

Bolan ran to the next black Caddy in line, saw the keys on the car seat and jumped inside. The rig started on the first twist of the key, and he raced after Nazarione. By the time the guard had opened the big gate at the end of the drive for his boss, Bolan had made up the fifty-yard lead. As the iron grillwork began to close, the Executioner's crew wagon screeched past it, scraping the side of the Caddy, but charging forward after the other black car.

The Caddies screamed through the posh residential section, then down a hill into a more modest area. Soon they careered through a small deserted industrial park. Bolan found a safe spot to shoot the big .44 and put one shot through the crew wagon's rear window and a second through the left rear tire.

His next blast punctured another tire, and the big rig swerved but continued through the industrial area, stopping beside a vacant lot. Two doors popped open and two figures ran across the lot toward a traveling carnival that had set up on the far side of the field next to a shopping center.

The Executioner jumped the curb with the Caddy and drove into the field until he reached a large ditch. He bailed out and ran after the pair, but saw he could not reach them before they entered the midway.

By the time Bolan ran to the big trailers that opened into carnival attractions, he saw Nazarione and his driver rush past a ticket taker into the fun house.

Bolan charged forward, said, "Police," to the ticket taker and hurried after them.

It was a slow night. Only two teenagers were inside the first room, inspecting themselves in the skinny-fat mirrors. The door closest to the entrance swung toward him and Bolan guessed the Mafia hardman and his boss had gone through it. He crouched as he followed, and two shots snarled over him in the darkness.

The area was as black as a Mafia don's heart. A soft recorded voice pleaded with them to save the fair maiden from the villain who was about to terrorize her.

Bolan held absolutely still, listening.

He wondered if this was a room or just a narrow passage. A strobe light shattered the darkness with its pulsating beam, but it came only three times. Before his eyes became accustomed to the change in light the strobe died. The Executioner had seen movement to his left. He had no idea how many people were in the room. More than the two goons?

He moved three steps forward.

Someone with a smoker's hack coughed ahead and to the right. Bolan took a coin from his pocket and flipped it so it would come down near where he thought someone crouched. The coin landed on the metal floor of the trailer louder than Bolan had hoped. The immediate response from the enemy was a pair of shots aimed at the sound.

The Executioner flipped the Beretta to 3-shot mode and drilled the blackness to the right of the place where the two muzzle-flashes showed. Before the echo of the two Mafia shots died in the room, someone screamed and fell hard to the floor.

A lighted ghoulish head popped out of the ceiling, braying a devilish laugh. A shaft of light appeared straight ahead, and a door creaked open. Bolan bolted for the door as it swung shut in the eerie light, which revealed a pair of teenagers trembling in one corner and the sprawled form of a man on the floor with a growing pool of dark-red blood forming under his chest.

Bolan swung the door open without going through it, heard a shot from the next room and a splintering sound as a slug ripped through the wood. Crouching, he went past the door and saw in the half light that the new room was peopled by a dozen frenzied wooden cutout figures, offering customers the chance to play any part in the wild and frenetic cast by standing behind the headless figures.

A head moved behind one of the cutouts and a .45 lifted. Bolan sent another burst of silent rounds at the arm and gun. Two of the parabellum rounds dug through Carlo Nazarione's wrist, and he screeched, dropped the .45 and rushed toward the far door.

A loudspeaker announced that there would now be a twelve-second period of total darkness for characters to change places or for lovers to kiss. The recording ended with a shriek of evil laughter and the sound of a creaking door.

The sudden darkness masked Nazarione as he darted around the wooden figures and ran into the next room.

Bolan worked his way to the door, eased it open and looked into the next room. It was fully lighted, and straight ahead he saw someone staring back at him. He was about to raise the Beretta when he realized it was his own reflection.

He slipped inside the hall of mirrors. Normally, the trick was to find your way through. Now there was a double trick—find your way through and not get shot. He was sure Nazarione would have a backup piece.

Before he could move, a handgun barked—a .38, it sounded like. He looked ahead to see his image in the mirror shattered by the round.

"Goddamn!" Nazarione shouted, and Bolan heard footsteps. He moved down the narrow passage, touching mirrors on both sides. He came to a turn. Ahead the mirrored passage bent at a forty-five-degree angle. Bolan checked but did not see Nazarione or any reflection of the don. He was not sure he could tell the difference.

Now he ran down the passage, almost slamming into the end, peering around, running again, rounding the next corner carefully. Seeing Nazarione staring at him, Bolan fired at once, an automatic reaction, only to see the image shatter and hear Nazarione's harsh laugh from somewhere to the right.

Bolan wished he could know for certain that there were no other people in the mirror maze. If that were the case, he would start shooting through the mirrors at sounds, not sights.

Again Bolan charged ahead, realizing the passages were turning back toward the beginning. He walked down an aisle and too late saw Nazarione pulling the trigger on his .38 automatic.

Bolan expected to feel the bite of hot lead; instead, a mirror shattered somewhere to his right. He heard Nazarione swearing and saw him running. Though he could see Nazarione and Nazarione could see him, neither was in the other's line of fire.

The Executioner heard a roar of anger from the Mafia don and saw him turn and fire. Bolan dropped to the floor as the gunman fired four rounds into the mirrored panels. Glass shattered over Bolan's head and to his right, then all was quiet.

"Give it up, Nazarione. You're out of rounds."

"The hell I am. I have plenty and I'm coming after you."

Bolan saw him dart out of sight. He listened. The sounds moved to the left, then to the right, then almost beside him. Bolan looked at the damaged mirrors in the passage beside him. Foot-square panels had shattered on both sides of the thin wall, and he could see into the next aisle. He pushed his hand through the void and looked ahead. He could see his hand reflected in the mirror at the end of the passage. He moved ahead stealthily, positioned himself firmly against the mirrors at the end of the passage and waited.

Carlo Nazarione moved noisily through the maze. Bolan stood where he was and waited.

A moment later Nazarione appeared at the end of the passage, raised his gun but did not fire.

"No way. Not again, Bolan. I'm going to wait until I can see you bleed your life away before I shoot you. I've killed enough of the damn mirrors. I want the real you. I'll blast you apart, then I'm gonna laugh."

Bolan's image at the far end of the hallway lifted its gun and stepped away from the mirror.

Nazarione gasped and jerked up his weapon. He was too late. Three rounds from the Beretta ripped into the Mafia don's chest, then three more slammed into his face as he pitched to the side, hit the mirrors and slid to the floor.

Bolan went out of the maze the way he had come in, walked through the weird cutout-character room, the black room and the main entrance.

He nodded to the ticket taker as he went out.

"Too scary for me," he said. His Beretta was under his shirt; Big Thunder, holster and all, was in his hand. He walked out of the carnival glad that the roaring sounds and shrieks of the sound effects in the fun house had covered the sounds of the shots.

The Executioner took a taxi back to his hotel. He would check in with Johnny at Strongbase One. Maybe he could even get back to San Diego for a week of deep-sea fishing. Maybe.

Mack Bolan inhaled deeply. Animal man was still out there, the Mafia was still clobbering the little guy, taking advantage of him. Until the Mafia was wiped out, Mack Bolan knew he would have no real rest.

As the taxi neared the hotel, a Baltimore Police Department squad car rushed by with red light flashing and siren blasting, on its way to a call at the traveling carnival fun house.

MORE ACTION!
MORE SUSPENSE!
NEW LOOK!

THE EXECUTIONER

MACK BOLAN

Beginning in July, watch out for America's number-one hero, Mack Bolan, in more spectacular, more gut-wrenching missions.

The Executioner continues to live large in bigger, bolder stories that can only be told in 256 pages.

Get into the heart of the man and the heart of the action with the first big entry, **The Trial**.

In this gripping adventure, Bolan is captured and placed on trial for his life—accused by the government he had sworn to serve. And the prosecution is hunting for the soldier's head.

Gold Eagle Books is giving readers what they asked for. You've never read action-adventure like this before!

AVAILABLE NOW!

Following the success of Dirty War comes SuperBolan #5

A routine flight departing Munich for New York
is forced to land at Beirut International Airport.

A whispered word echoes through the jumbo's cabin,
leaving panic and terror in its wake.

Hijack!

Aboard the giant silver bird the occupants silently
await their fate.

And among them is a special passenger. . . .

4 FREE BOOKS
1 FREE GIFT
NO RISK
NO OBLIGATION
NO KIDDING